ALPHA CLASS 04: GRADUATION

ALPHA CLASS 04: GRADUATION

ETHERIC ACADEMY

TS PAUL ND ROBERTS MICHAEL ANDERLE

DISRUPTIVE IMAGINATION

LMBPN Publishing
PMB 196, 2540 South Maryland Pkwy
Las Vegas, NV 89109

First US edition, March 2020

CHAPTER ONE

QBBS Meredith Reynolds, Medical Level, General Lobby

Guardian Commander Peter Silvers crossed the lobby on his way to check on Craig. The hush of the night shift reminded him a little of being in church when he was young.

Same peace, or something.

He nodded at Madeline as he passed her at the reception desk. The administrator smiled and wiggled her fingers at him before returning to work.

Peter took out his tablet while he waited for the elevator to arrive and replayed the captured footage the guys at the APA had sent him of Craig's latest failure to think before acting.

It wasn't that the newly-booted Guardian didn't have brains—he was damn smart for a wall of muscle—but Craig's failure to apply that intelligence in the heat of the moment was going to get someone killed. Probably himself.

It was time for him to grow up.

Peter left the elevator and made his way to the ward to which Craig had been taken for observation. He checked the room number, put his tablet away, and knocked softly before entering.

Craig looked up as Peter came in. "Sir?"

Peter picked up Craig's chart and sat in the chair by his bed. "We need to have a talk."

Craig's head dropped. "About me losing to the Chinese team?"

"No. About you assuming you'd win because you're a Wechselbalg. And about you being foolish enough to give away your advantage for the sake of bragging rights."

Craig was confused. "I don't get it, sir."

Peter held the chart up. "That's because you took eighteen—no, make that nineteen, they found another when they got you in here—tranq darts. That's thirteen more than they would have shot you with if you hadn't had such a big mouth. I'm surprised you're even awake."

Craig sat up and put a hand to his head. "Yeah, well, I learned my lesson."

Peter put the chart back at the end of the bed. "I'd love to believe that, but unfortunately, I know you." He sighed. "Look...you have the potential to be one of the best, but it's not gonna happen if you keep doing stupid shit. I'm putting you on probation."

"But, sir!"

Peter shook his head. "No buts. You need to shape up, and until you do you're off active duty." He held up a hand to stay Craig's protest. "You'll be assigned to me until you don't need a babysitter anymore. Seriously, if you would just take the time to think before–"

Meredith pinged Peter, saving Craig from his lecture–for now. "I have to take this," he told Craig. "I'll see you tomorrow, bright and early. You got enough sleep today, right?"

He left Craig's room, speaking to Meredith as he made his way back to the elevator. *What's up?*

There is a situation in the psychiatric wing. I thought you should know.

You thought? Peter asked, heading for the psych wing.

You know very well what I meant, she chided. *It was appropriate to inform you, and I attempted to do so in a more human fashion to put you at ease. If it is a problem, I shall refrain from doing so in the future.*

I'm just riding you. Practice away. Peter chuckled, getting his tablet out again as he stepped aboard the elevator. *Show me what's happening.*

The screen lit up to show a room Peter didn't recognize and a man wearing a hospital gown fighting valiantly against six orderlies. *Where is this?*

Meredith brought up a map of the level. *He's currently on Ward G.*

Well, he's not going to be there for long if he takes all the orderlies out. Dude's got moves, that's for sure. Put the live feed back on; let me see if they've managed to contain him.

Meredith switched back to the ward's cameras. Peter sucked a breath in when he saw that the man had incapacitated all the orderlies. *Are they okay?*

Yes, Meredith replied. *They are unconscious but alive.*

The man's head swung to the left and right, his hyper-aware gaze alighting on the open door. The next moment a wolf stood in the man's place, sandy-furred and broad across the shoulders.

The wolf broke for the door.

Meredith—

We're there now, the EI cut in as the elevator doors opened on the lobby. *I have requested that additional orderlies be dispatched, and they are on their way.*

Peter strode out of the elevator on full alert. The lobby was completely silent now. Even Madeline had packed up and left for the night.

Where is our wolf?

Approaching from the west corridor, she told him. *The orderlies I requested are in pursuit.*

Before Peter had a chance to reply a sandy blur shot out of the corridor leading to the psych wing, closely followed by a bunch of orderlies with tranquilizer guns drawn.

Peter chuckled. *I guess this guy won't be* walking *back to his ward,* he quipped when he spotted another two orderlies coming up the corridor pushing a gurney.

Is that really a laughing matter? Meredith asked. *How will I ever get the hang of humor if the boundaries keep shifting?*

The lead orderly was relieved when she saw Peter. She gestured for him to cover the exits while her team fanned out to prevent the Were from escaping farther into the medical level.

Peter swerved to intercept the Were, vaulting over the benches toward the revolving doors as the armed orderlies skidded to a halt and unloaded their tranquilizer darts into the rear end of the panicked wolf.

The darts didn't slow the Were down. If anything, he

was spurred on by the pain. He yelped when they hit his hindquarters and hurtled even faster toward the exit, unheeding of Peter standing between him and his freedom.

Peter hesitated for a split second. He didn't want to hurt the Were; he wasn't an enemy, just a sick man.

"Don't let him get out," one of the orderlies called.

I've locked the main doors, Meredith told him. *You just need to make sure he doesn't leave by the access ramp.*

Peter altered his course again, placing himself between the open ramp and the wolf. *Thanks, Meredith.*

Don't thank me yet. I calculate it'll be another two minutes before the tranquilizers take effect. You may have to restrain him.

Peter agreed. The drugs were beginning to take effect, but not fast enough. He held his position as the Were almost lost his footing, his claws skittering on the smooth stone. Then he gained purchase and pelted toward the exit with the hospital gown flapping around him. He finally saw Peter blocking his way and leapt to the side to evade capture.

Gott Verdammt, *he's not going to give me a choice!*

He winced at the choked cough the Were made when he slammed chest-first into Peter's outstretched arm and dropped.

Peter prepared himself to take a rough dive as the Were hauled himself to shaky paws and shook his head sluggishly. He thought the wolf was about to bolt again, but the hospital gown he was somehow still wearing finally slipped all the way down and tangled in his front legs, tripping him. Peter grimaced as the half-conscious wolf lost

5

his equilibrium altogether and crashed face-first into the bench.

The wolf was gone the next minute, replaced by a sturdy and heavily-scarred man with a bushy beard. The orderlies were already there and two began removing the darts from his rear end, while the other two with the gurney prepared it to transfer him.

The man moaned and mumbled incoherently as they moved him and strapped him in securely. "You cannot keep me...you... You must let me go to him... *Let me go...*"

A female orderly tucked a blanket around the naked man as he slipped from consciousness. "There, now. We've got you."

Peter ran a hand over his head, grimacing as he saw the bruising on the man's chest. "Is he gonna be okay, um...?"

The orderly smiled at Peter as she fastened a strap across the gurney. "Thanks for the assist. Dionne." She held out a hand, which Peter shook. "Yeah, he's not ready to be out unsupervised yet." She attached a clip to the patient's finger. "He keeps trying to get out, no matter what we do. This is the second time we've had to restrain him today."

Peter frowned in sympathy. "Who was he asking for just then? His family?"

Dionne shook her head sadly. "We have no idea. We don't even know his real name. He came up here with an old woman in one of the first evacuations. She called him 'Ilya' for lack of anything else."

"She's not his mother?"

"No, just some woman who found him near-dead at the edge of her farm and took him in. He's been here, oh, let me see...over a year, anyway. It's a sad story, really, but we're doing what we can for him and he's on the road to recovery. We hope that his nanos will repair the injuries and he'll get his memory back."

"Can't the Pod-doc heal him?"

Dionne shook her head. "The Pod-doc repaired the structure of his neural pathways, but that's as much as it can do. He had a serious brain trauma, if he hadn't had nanocytes then he wouldn't have even made it this far. He can function day-to-day but his memory is shot, for want of a better phrase, until we can help him re-establish the connections."

Peter sucked in a breath. "Poor guy."

She nodded her agreement. "It's not hopeless. He's usually pretty calm, but he's been having episodes like this more frequently as his treatment helps him to remember. The problem is that the memories return out of order, often with no context. He has manic episodes; his latest is that believes he's back on Earth looking for someone. Like I said, not hopeless, it's actually a sign of recovery. Our main concern is keeping him safe until he regains control of himself."

Peter frowned. "And you have *no* idea who he is?"

"Not a clue. The woman didn't know anything about him. He's strong for a Wechselbalg. He might be able to tell us something once he gets some more of his memory back, but that can't be rushed. I can tell you one thing: he's a *hell* of a fighter." She nodded and bent to push the gurney at her end. "Thanks again, Commander."

Peter nodded in return. "'Peter' is fine. Keep me informed, please. I want to know if this happens again. In the meantime, I'll assign a couple of Guardians to be here

7

in case he gets out again. I'll also ask around, see if I can find anyone who might know who he is."

Dionne nodded. "That would be great."

Peter lost himself in thought as the orderlies pushed the gurney away. He couldn't imagine the torment the man was going through. To have nothing left of his mind but the compulsion to find someone whom he couldn't even remember? That had to be tearing him apart at the deepest level. He wondered who "Ilya" was searching for.

Who could be so dear to him that even the brain trauma he'd suffered couldn't completely wipe him from his memory?

CHAPTER TWO

Q BBS *Meredith Reynolds*, Etheric Academy, Administrators' Office

The puppy was curled on her bed in the corner of the office. She let out a sleepy snuffle, all four paws moving as she gave chase in her dreams.

Diane was distracted, tapping a finger on her lips. "When we agreed to take Devi in I never considered that we'd be too busy watching her sleep to get any work done. She's no trouble at all; such a sweetheart."

"Especially now she's had the same enhancements as Matrix and can talk to us properly. Who would have thought a dog would improve our lives this much?" Dorene smiled as she watched Devi sleep.

"Hmm?" Diane dragged her gaze away from the dog bed. "I'll miss her when we reopen. But she has an inquisitive mind when she's not busy accessorizing. Having her around will make the students feel safe, especially after the attacks." Diane shook her head, "Can you believe jihadi terrorists attacked us all the way out *here?*"

Dorene nodded. "Yes, completely. Although I think I was more terrorized by the sight of Bobcat's backside pressed against the window than those idiots in the caskets." She shuddered. "*Ugh*. I can't repress the sight of that video no matter how much I try!"

Diane cracked up at that. "What's the matter, DJ? Was the moon too bright for you?"

Dorene gave her twin a sour look. "You know it was, dear. Now back to business, if you're all done? There's been enough to do just getting ready to go through the Gate. Did Max and Van agree to help out with the kids?"

Diane nodded. "They're making preparations as we speak. Max may need to be reined in a little. The last I saw him, he was shepherding a flock of antigrav pallets to the auditorium. When I asked him what he was up to, he said the least we could do while the men and women of the fleet protect our people is to provide a pleasant place to stay for their kids while they do it."

"That man is an absolute treasure. We'll go visit him shortly and see what we can do to help. But first, Devi's protection vest has arrived and she needs to try it on for size."

"She's not going to be happy about it, DJ."

"Don't I know it," Dorene replied. She pulled a silver-wrapped box out from under her desk and began undoing the bow on the top. "She's doing very well in her training, and I have faith she'll be a good guardian for the school. She just needs some time to adjust to wearing her uniform before she has to wear it every day."

Devi's ears twitched at the rustle of tissue paper, but her eyes remained shut.

Diane lowered her voice. "You know as well as I do how we're going to get Devi to wear that vest. We'll reward her for being *brave*. None of Bellatrix' and Ashur's puppies like wearing this stuff, but I think something shiny might help get our girl motivated." She nodded at the box on her sister's desk. "I'm guessing you've already thought of that?"

Dorene passed her sister one of the tissue-wrapped packages from the box with a wink. "You guessed right. I had a visit from one of ADAM's fashionistas this morning and she dropped off our order."

Diane peeked inside the tissue paper. "I think this might just do the trick, DJ." She turned to the puppy. "Devi, sweetheart, we got you a gift."

Devi jumped up at the sound of her name and trotted sleepily over to the desks. She sat in front of Diane and Dorene with her tongue lolling out and yawned. "A gift? What is it? Is it treats?"

"Better than treats, sweetheart," Diane answered.

"Is it pretties?" Devi's ears perked up and she yipped with excitement. "I *love* pretties!"

Diane smiled and held up a stiff puppy-shaped protection vest. "But to get the pretties, you have to try your new vest on before we leave for the auditorium."

Devi looked up at her humans. "It's not very sparkly, is it?" She nosed the matte black material. "I want to look pretty for my first day at school. Mother always says it's important to make a good first impression." Devi turned her back and looked away. "Won't. It's not pretty, and it will pinch me like the last one did." She snorted her disapproval in case her bonded humans were unclear about her feelings.

11

Dorene unwrapped one of the tissue paper packages, revealing a sparkly clip-on tie in Academy colors. "It could be worse. Bethany Anne could have said you have to wear full armor like your brothers. The vest isn't negotiable, Devi, but if you stop all this and turn around, you'll see all the accessories we got to go with it!"

Devi's nose twitched, but she didn't turn her head. "Are those sequins I smell?"

"You'll have to stop sulking and try on your vest to find out," Dorene told the recalcitrant puppy, quickly wrapping the tie up again. "I promise the vest won't pinch. We made sure this one will grow with you–for a while, at least. Sweetheart, it's important to us that you have some protection when school starts. You're not just there to learn, you're also guarding the students."

"When you say it that way it makes more sense." Devi huffed and hopped up to rest her front paws on Diane's knees. "Very well, I will try it on, but *then* I get the pretties, right?"

"Of course." Diane chuckled as she fastened the straps underneath Devi. "All done."

She shook her fur and let out a little chuff. "It doesn't pinch, but I can't make a good impression dressed in *this*! It doesn't even match my pet-icure!" She held up a paw to show Diane five glittery purple claws.

"Very nice! Did one of the students do that for you?"

"It was Mischa." Devi's tail thumped. "I like Masha and Mischa." Her head swiveled at the sound of crinkling tissue paper. "Are those my pretties?"

Dorene pulled out the sparkly tie and a pair of matching bows and held them up for the puppy to see.

Devi gave her humans a doggy grin. "Now that's more like it! Are they from ADAM? His bows don't pinch like the ones from the pet store." She raised her head so Dorene could clip the tie onto her collar, being careful of the translation device that was fixed to it so she could talk to anyone who didn't have a chip.

"They are," Dorene assured her before pressing the bows gently to her ears. "He also told me his team has improved the adhesive so they can be re-worn."

Diane scratched the top of her head. "You look adorable, Devi. Are you ready to make a big splash at school?"

"I was ready weeks ago!" Devi danced in a circle, chuffing as her tie flapped. "I don't want to wait. I want excitement! I want to learn!" She flopped down and rolled over with a dramatic sigh.

Dorene tsked. "Now, Devi, we're about to leave our solar system and travel to a new one. Surely that's enough excitement?"

Devi sniffed noncommittally. "I suppose so."

"That's our good girl," Diane cooed. "Let's go see how everyone likes your pretties. It's time."

Devi wagged her tail and went ahead, checking that the way ahead was clear for her humans as they walked to the auditorium, just as she'd been trained.

Diane and Dorene gasped when they opened the doors. The auditorium had been transformed. An enormous holo-banner hanging above the stage drew their attention first, the current scene shifting from a superhero-style line-up of Bethany Anne and her Bitches to an animated depiction of the *Meredith Reynolds* flying through the Annex Gate in a burst of sparkles.

Dorene pointed at the banner. *"That* is out of this world. What on earth is Max doing? And is that popcorn I smell?"

They headed over to the stage, where the grandfatherly custodian was conducting the teachers. His bushy mustache danced as he shouted directions whilst assembling some contraption on the stage beneath the holobanner, which now read *'Happy Exodus Day!'* in rippling neon light.

The sisters wandered through the large open space that had been created in front of the stage by removing the seating rows. The Academy faculty were there in full force, setting up sectioned areas for the expected children. The stage lights alternated bright colors, the fairy-light effect reflected all over the auditorium by the giant disco ball that had been suspended from the ceiling. Decorations were affixed to every available surface, along with balloons and bunting that stretched from wall to wall.

"You weren't kidding when you said Max was running with this," Dorene remarked dryly. "Is that...a dancefloor?

"I believe it is." Diane smiled when they reached the foot of the stage. "The man's done good, sis. Hey, Maestro," Diane called up to him. "What *is* all this?"

Max spread his arms wide, grinning from ear to ear. "It's great, isn't it? Everyone who was free came to pitch in when they heard we were babysitting during the crossing. They all wanted to do their part to help."

He pointed out the various areas being set up. "Soft play for the little ones, sleeping area for when they need naps, dance floor over there with the arcade games for the older kids. Chef Van is setting up a finger-food buffet near the back." He indicated the soft projection screens mounted behind him in the alcove at the rear of the stage. "Tina, Ron, and Aleksei set up a live feed of the fleet with Meredith's help. She was already providing access for their dorm party, so it wasn't a bother. All that's left is arranging some comfortable seating."

The sisters drank it all in as they joined Max on the stage.

Max's expression grew serious for a moment. "None of the kids will have time to dwell on their parents—not on *my* watch. Besides, this is a big day for humanity, ladies. We should be celebrating!"

Devi looked up at her bonded humans. "Are you two okay? Why are your eyes leaking?"

"Look at how they all came together, Devi." Diane sniffed.

Dorene dabbed her eye with a tissue. "That's what we do, dear. Humanity's biggest strength is the way we pull together under pressure." She squared her shoulders, seeing one of the new teachers struggling under a full armload of party supplies. "Looks like Katie needs a hand. Come on, let's go help her."

Diane was already halfway down the steps. "You don't have to ask *me* twice!"

QBBS *Meredith Reynolds*, Etheric Academy, Alpha Class Dormitory

Tina inhaled the aroma of the pizza on her plate

happily as she snuggled down into the sofa between Yana and Ron, humming the theme to *Star Journey* as she waited for the first ship to cross the Annex Gate. The Alpha Class dorm was comfortably overfull, which was just how she liked it.

The events in Wales before the school break had changed the class dynamic. Their tightly-knit group had expanded to include Aleksei, Halli, and the twins, who spent more time with Alpha class than they did their own classmates these days. Even Craig occasionally found time after his Guardian training to hang out with them all.

We strengthen each other, Tina thought. The party was only missing Craig and Halli, and she wished they'd hurry up before they missed the event of a lifetime.

They'd cleared the wall to use as a screen for the projectors Tina, Ron, and Aleksei had set up. The wide off-white space was now covered with windows which showed multiple angles of the fleet gathered at the Annex Gate. The window showing the Annex Gate took up the biggest space in the center of the wall, surrounded by smaller windows showing the remaining feeds in rotation.

Bai Hu bounced about on the sofa next to Yana. He spilled his popcorn on the twins, who were slouched on the beanbag arguing with Nestor and Maxim over the space on the floor between the sofa and the table. Everyone wanted to be close to the food.

Aleksei sat off to the side with his tablet in hand, playing with the fleet data as it came in on the feeds Meredith had granted them access to. "Hey, quit it! The order to get ready has been given."

Halli, out of breath, burst into the dorm and threw

ALPHA CLASS 04: GRADUATION

herself on the sofa next to Ron. "Craig made it off probation. He's back on duty."

Maxim grinned. He'd had fun ribbing Craig about his probation but he was glad to hear it was over. "Do you know which ship he's stationed on?"

"The *Coach's Revenge*." She tapped Nestor on the shoulder and pointed at the table. "Food, please. Has it started? Did I miss it?"

"No, you're just in time," Maxim told her, leaning back to pass her a bowl of popcorn from the table.

Aleksei waved frantically. "The order to advance has been given!"

Tina linked her arms through Yana's and Ron's and squeezed tight. "This is it!" she squealed. "Our very own *Star Journey*!"

"*Space, the ultimate unknown*," Ron intoned.

Tina didn't miss a beat. "*This is the journey of...*the Etheric Empire,"

Yana chipped in, "Bethany Anne's eternal mission…"

The twins were next.

"To leave…"

"The mudball…"

"Behind."

"To seek out the Kurtherians," Halli interjected.

Maxim and Nestor shouted at the same time, "And kick their slimy asses…"

"Right back to the Big Bang!" Alexi concluded with a fist-pump.

They collapsed in fits of laughter, including Bai Hu, who had been watching *Star Journey* with the group and for once got the reference.

"It's starting!" Yana cried.

"To space!" Bai Hu yelled, jumping up and down on the sofa again in his excitement.

Silence fell as the humans' fleet advanced toward the Annex Gate.

The first ships entered the Gate, causing the waves within the green circle to shimmer in an opalescent rainbow.

The exodus had begun.

The fleet sailed into the unknown, leaving everything they had known behind. Every soul aboard the ships of the Etheric Empire was filled to bursting with one purpose and one purpose only: to defend Earth from any species that sought to harm the human race.

"*Ad Aeternitatem.*" Maxim breathed the oath, utterly captivated by the coordinated approach of so many vessels.

He saw the *G'laxix Sphaea* bringing up the rear, and other Sphaea-class ships holding their positions around the *Meredith Reynolds*, along with many others. The Black Eagles and the Puck Destroyers he recognized, but most of the rest he did not. "Where is the *Coach's Revenge*?"

Aleksei tapped his tablet. "Window eight. We are approaching the Gate."

The feeds flickered for a few moments before stabilizing once the *Meredith Reynolds* had egressed.

They cheered when they saw the *G'laxix Sphaea* emerge from the Yollin side of the Gate, jumping up and spilling popcorn everywhere. Maxim grabbed Nestor in a crushing hug and spun him around. "We made it!"

Then the impossible happened.

The feeds flickered again.

Ten mouths dropped open as the way back to Earth disintegrated before their eyes. An explosion from the Sol side pulverized the Gate on the Yollin side, the force creating a blast wave that flung the wreckage out toward the stars.

Nobody said a word. They couldn't. Horrified silence grew thick in the air as chunks of the ruined Gate floated by on the wall displays.

Bai Hu was the first to break it, jumping up into a defensive crouch on the sofa. His eyes began to glow. "*Jiějiě,* what is happening?"

Yana didn't answer. She shook her head, a single tear tracking down her ashen cheek as she stared blankly at the feeds. Bai Hu looked around frantically, searching for an answer from one of the others.

"The Gate went '*boom,*' Bai Hu," Tina whispered.

Ron snorted. "It didn't go *boom*. Nothing in space goes *boom*. It can't; it's a vacuum."

Tina looked at him in disbelief. "Now is *not* the time to be pedantic, Ron!"

"Oh, please, don't start, you two," Mischa moaned. "What's going on? What happened to the Gate?"

Aleksei shrugged. "It's gone."

"That is it," Maxim whispered hoarsely. "We will never see Earth again. My father... Now I will never know what happened to him."

Nestor reached out to his cousin. "I am so sorry, my brother. I had also hoped we would find Uncle Nikolai."

Maxim stared at him with yellowing eyes, unseeing. "I... I can't do this. I have to go." He shook himself free of Nestor and ran from the dorm.

"Wait!" Nestor cried, starting after him.

"What is wrong with Maxim?" Bai Hu whispered to Yana, holding tight to her arm.

Yana stroked her brother's head. "Shhh, *Kotenok*. He is grieving for his father, who he will probably never see again" she replied quietly. She looked at the others. "I think we should all go and help in the auditorium with the children. They will be afraid for their parents." She shooed Bai Hu toward the door. "Come along."

Masha and Mischa had continued to watch the devastation unfold, oblivious to the tension in the dorm. They tore themselves away from the feeds and followed Yana and Bai Hu in stunned silence.

Aleksei remained glued to his tablet, his head bobbing as he looked at the displays on the wall. "I don't think we've taken any losses. All the ships are still there."

Ron raised his eyebrows in disbelief. "You didn't count them all!"

"I did, before we went through the Gate and after it exploded." Aleksei shrugged and let out a strange chuckle. "As long as nobody died, I guess it's not that big of a deal. It's not like we're stuck here forever."

Tina rounded on him. "Wow, Aleksei! If stupid was dirt you'd cover an acre. We are stranded with no way of getting back to Earth and it's 'not that big a deal?' I expect Craig to come out with stupid stuff like that, but not you."

Aleksei looked hurt. "I didn't mean it like that. Why are you being so mean?"

Ron looked pained and patted Aleksei on the back. "Yeah, that was way too snarky, Tina. It's not Aleksei's fault, so calm down!"

Tina's mouth fell open and she looked at Ron incredulously, her fists clenching involuntarily. "Calm down? *Calm down?* You *did* just see our only way home get blown to pieces, right? I'm going to the auditorium to help." She pointed at Ron. "*You* should go somewhere else. *Anywhere else!*"

She stormed out, leaving Ron and Aleksei in stunned silence. They looked at each other and shrugged.

"It's not like we can do anything about it," Aleksei protested. "BMW will get us back to the mudball. She shouldn't worry."

"Try telling *her* that," Ron argued.

Aleksei shook his head solemnly. "I would never dream of doing that. My father told me that the greatest advice he could ever give me was to never tell an angry woman anything. I am coming to believe the truth of it."

As the door slammed behind Tina they heard her final words on the subject.

"UGH! *BOYS!*"

CHAPTER THREE

QBBS Meredith Reynolds, Etheric Academy, PET Annex

Maxim's eyes stung and the tears he held back blurred the corridors of the Academy as he tried to outrun his grief. He wanted one more minute–just a second, even–of believing that he would see his father again. Denied that, he wanted to hit something repeatedly until his knuckles were as bruised as his heart.

He swerved around two girls who were just leaving the annex, catching the door they held for him with a gruff acknowledgment as he hurried inside. The corridor around Maxim had a yellow sheen as his emotions disturbed his focus, so he forced them down and channeled the energy into an extra burst of speed.

I will not lose my hold on my wolf!

He charged into the student APA, his only concern finding release before the torrent of emotion was all that was left of him. He almost sobbed with relief to see that the room was empty and veered over to the nearest vacant punching bag.

"*Grrrraaagghh!*" His fists hit the leather over and over. The pain of his unwrapped knuckles splitting under the power he put into his punches went unnoticed, insignificant compared to the pain inside.

He was utterly alone.

The loss of the Annex Gate meant the destruction of the final tenuous hope he had held of being reunited with his father. His fantasies of Nikolai being found had been dashed into as many pieces as the Annex Gate.

I will never be able to look him in the eye and tell him how his sacrifice shaped the man I am becoming. He will never see my future children or know that the love he had for me will make me strong enough to protect the weak in the years to come.

Maxim's tears fell freely and he kept pounding the bag, forcing the pain of the present to retreat as he lost himself in memories of the time when he and his father had been inseparable.

As deeply as he loved his cousin and uncle, nothing could replace the bond he and his dad had shared.

"Hey, buddy, you want to give your hands a break? You're bleeding all over the mat there."

Maxim jerked at the interruption, startled from the rhythmic trance he had worked himself into. Guardian Commander Peter Silvers, who was behind him, held out a clean towel and looked at Maxim with a mixture of sadness and concern.

Maxim glanced down at his tattered knuckles and took the towel from Peter. "Sorry for the mess, sir."

Peter chuckled. "Don't worry about it. I'm impressed

that you were able to get down here and work out your issue on the bag instead of going wolf and tearing up the Academy. When Meredith alerted me, I expected to use the trail of destruction to lead me to you."

Maxim frowned and wiped the blood from his hands even as his nanocytes healed the damage. "I would not lose control like that. My wolf is my responsibility."

Peter regarded him for a moment, not missing the rapidity with which the young man's knuckles were healing—or his stoic acceptance of the crushing news. "I think I see why John asked me to do some work with you. Do you wanna talk about it?"

Maxim shook his head. "There is nothing to discuss. The Annex Gate is gone and we are never going to see Earth again. I am not the only one who has lost their family." He sighed. "I find it hard to bear that I will never know my father's fate."

Peter laid a hand on Maxim's shoulder. "From what I've heard, Nikolai's selflessness saved a lot of lives. Did you know that a lot of people joined the Guardians after your group arrived from Siberia? They all told the story of your evacuation and they all praised your dad. None of them saw him die, Maxim. There's every chance he's still alive back on Earth."

Maxim shrugged Peter's hand off; it was time to face the facts. "If he was alive, ADAM would have found him. I already knew, really. Now I just have to accept it."

"I think I can help with that," Peter told him. "I want you to go and see a friend of mine, Doc Dietrich. He usually deals with combat trauma—it's kind of his thing—but I think you'll find it good to talk about this with him."

Maxim's nose wrinkled. "I don't know. I'll try if you think it would help, sir."

Peter was amazed that Maxim had been able to regain his composure despite the grief he was clearly wrestling with. "You're a wise young man, Maxim Nikolayevich." He tossed the boy a roll of tape. "I don't think there are many Wechselbalg–even adults–who would have been able to maintain control like you did today. You're going to make a great Guardian. Wrap your hands, then we'll spar for a while. We need to discuss your training."

Maxim nodded, following Peter's instruction. "Thank you, sir."

Peter grinned as Maxim tossed the tape back. "No need to thank me. Now get your guard up."

CHAPTER FOUR

Q BBS *Meredith Reynolds*, Etheric Academy, Science Wing, a Few Weeks Later

Masha had first-day blues.

The start of school had been delayed due to the Yollin revolution, but there was no avoiding it any longer.

She felt she'd outgrown the Academy, but her parents would hear none of it. She hadn't argued too much, knowing that what was waiting for her after graduation would be just as unsatisfying to her as sitting in a classroom. It wasn't that being a Guardian wasn't good enough, as her father had assumed when she'd tried to explain, but she wanted a bigger life than that of a soldier. She *wanted* to serve—just in her own way.

She lagged behind Mischa and the others, lost in thought as they arrived at the doors to the Science Wing. Yana ground to a halt and pulled out her tablet. She pointed it at the quote above the doors. "One minute. Tina loves these, and I said I'd send her photos of the new ones."

Masha grumbled, "We'll be late for class." She looked up anyway.

'The task is not so much to see what no one has yet seen, but to think what nobody has yet thought about that which everybody sees.'

Masha scoffed to herself as she stalked into the classroom ahead of the others. *Yeah, right. All I do is think about things differently, so why is it that there's nowhere for someone like me to shine?*

The classroom seemed crowded with new students, although according to Aleksei fewer than ten percent of the emigrant children had passed the rigorous Academy entry exam. There were also few familiar faces in the room.

Her sister came over to sit next to her on the bench and chatted animatedly to Yana and Halli, who sat farther along the same row. Devi came in behind the last of the students and jumped onto one of the new Yollin chairs at the end.

Devi was the most interesting thing about school, as far as Masha was concerned. The puppy had a fabulous sense of style, if a little heavy on sparkles for her taste. She and Mischa had found common ground with the fashion-conscious German Shepherd as soon as they'd met, when Devi had noticed her sparkly purple nails and her sister had happened to have the bottle of ultraviolet sparkle polish she was wearing in her purse.

One pedicure–or *pet*-icure, as they now called them–later, the twins had a new best friend.

The teacher came in, tablet in hand. Masha noted her straight spine, direct gaze, and no-nonsense demeanor.

She sat up a little straighter and paid attention.

"Good morning, class!" The teacher pointed to the slide that appeared on the holographic interface behind her when she tapped her tablet. "As you can see, my name is Ms. Katie Treble. Welcome to the Genetic Engineering Taster Module. Those of you who enjoy this module will be able to enroll in the full course after graduation, but during this term, we will focus on the applications of genetic engineering for a space-faring species—namely us."

The class tittered at her humor.

"Very well, let's begin. Open your tablets to the first page of your text."

Masha opened the e-text for the class and skimmed the first page, which looked dry as dust. She sighed as the lesson began, not for the first time wishing she could be anywhere else but in school.

Ms. Treble paced as she spoke in an animated voice. "Genetically modified organisms, or GMOs, have been one of the most controversial topics of the modern era. Disregarding the debates back on Earth, genetic engineering is a cornerstone of humanity's continued survival. Our survival in space will rely heavily on the continually developing techniques and processes our scientists dream up."

She stopped pacing and faced the class. "We have developed grains that are drought- and disease-resistant, and others that are super-saturated with vital nutrients. We are able to breed food animals that grow faster and produce more calories for the same cost, and save endangered species from extinction. Genetic engineering will give humanity the ability to tame our environment."

Masha rolled her eyes. "Humanity abuses the mudball.

That's not taming, it's exploitation. Will we exploit the resources of the planets we find?"

Ms. Treble grinned and pointed at Masha. "You know, I was promised students who challenge everything, and you don't disappoint! First of all, let me assure you all that every proposed genetics project has to pass a rigorous ethical examination before it can be approved. This is not Earth, where an unscrupulous scientist can find a wealthy patron with questionable motives. Let me ask a question... How many of you are Wechselbalg?"

The twins raised their hands, along with Halli and a boy in the front row.

Ms. Treble smiled. "Without genetic engineering, there would *be* no Wechselbalg. There would be no vampires, so no Queen to lead us—and nobody to stand between Earth and the Kurtherians. Our military would be less powerful, our food supplies would be uncertain, and our medical capabilities would be much poorer. Without genetic engineering, the Battle for Yoll could not have been won, and humankind would have become slaves to the Kurtherian masquerading as their king."

She clicked her tablet and the slide changed to show an angora rabbit peering out from under its fluffy mop. "But those are the big concerns. There are many everyday applications for genetic engineering that would surprise you. Meet Boomer. Boomer and his herd are a sustainable economic source of natural fibers for our clothing manufacturers."

Halli raised her hand. "Why don't we just use sheep?"

The teacher grinned. "Great question, Halli. Why do you think we might have chosen rabbits over sheep?"

Halli frowned, thinking. "They're smaller?"

Ms. Treble nodded. "That's one reason. Can anyone else think of another?" A few hands went up and she pointed to them one at a time.

"They eat less than sheep do?"

"They poop less?"

"Sheep are harder to take care of?"

"They smell better?"

Ms. Treble held up a hand. "Good guesses. The answer is a combination of all those things. They are also hypoallergenic. However, our angoras are labor-intensive compared to most rabbit breeds."

Mischa raised her hand. "What do rabbits have to do with genetic engineering?"

"Why, everything!" Ms. Treble replied, switching the slide again to show a simple life-cycle diagram. "Angora rabbits shed their wool every ninety days or so. Boomer's DNA has been slightly altered to give him a denser coat and a shorter shedding cycle. We'll be studying Boomer's descendants to chart the progression of the altered gene in the rabbit population and sharing the results of the data collection with Bernadette and her team, so they know which rabbits to breed."

Yana raised her hand. "Why don't we just put them in the Pod-doc?"

"We could," Ms. Treble told them. "But it would be a waste of resources to alter each animal separately. Besides, the Pod-docs are reserved for military and medical use only. This is where we come in: we're going to assist the rabbit handlers to identify the rabbits with the modified gene. Later in the week, we'll be visiting the rabbit habitat to assist the handlers with grooming. Before we can work with the rabbits they have to get used to us, because stress can make them sick. Grooming them will help us avoid that."

The class murmured their appreciation for the project.

Ms. Treble grinned. "I'm glad you're all so engaged. Right, class. Before we get to data collation, we need to know what we are looking for. Turn to Chapter One of your texts, *Mendel's Principles of Inheritance...*'"

QBBS *Meredith Reynolds*, Open Court

Tina and Ron sat in a booth by the window in the diner. The open court was busy with people grabbing lunch, shopping, or just catching up, but Tina didn't notice any of it.

Her mind was on more serious matters.

She pushed her spoon into her half-finished dessert and looked out of the window. "I don't really want this."

"I'll make it disappear for you," Ron told her with a wink. He pulled her dish over next to his empty one and got to work demolishing the ice cream. "So, what was so important that we had to come all the way out here to talk about it?"

She made a face. "I have a decision to make–or more accurately, I've made a decision and I'm trying to figure out how to implement it."

Ron glanced up at her. "What kind of decision?"

"A big one. I have to switch my focus. Biology isn't where I'm needed." She picked up a paper napkin and began twisting off small pieces. "When you think of how little time has passed and how much has happened..." She shook her head, trying to find a way to encapsulate the events of the last few years.

Ron frowned in sympathy. "I know what you mean."

"Do you? Really?" She looked at the remains of the napkin on the table, then brushed them into her hand and deposited them on her empty plate. "Yoll...it made every-thing we did back on the mudball look like child's play."

Ron snickered. "It kind of was, if you think about it."

"Don't be an ass. What happened in Wales was *Gott Verdammt* serious, Ron." She sighed. "People *died*, and more people would have died without the defenses we built. The siege was when I realized that I have more to give. My work saved some of those lives. Now we're smack in the middle of the galactic stage and *everyone* is looking at us."

"Let them look." Ron shrugged. "It's all they'll be allowed to do."

Tina shook a finger at him, her face serious. "You know as well as I do that most of the new species we encounter will have to be taught to respect us. There's war ahead, and I can't justify playing around with bacteria—no matter how interesting it is—when I could be working toward the protection of our people. I just can't."

"I get it, really," Ron sympathized. "And I know we're going to make a difference. So what are you going to do if you're dropping biology?"

Tina grinned. "I spoke with Dorene about switching tracks and got her advice about my options, but I'm worried about what my mom will think. And say. You saw how badly she freaked at John and Jean when we got back from the UK."

"Well, yeah. She could have lost you. I wish my mom and dad worried that much. They probably wouldn't have even noticed if I'd died during any of our scrapes since starting school. It's like I've already grown up and left home."

Tina pressed her lips together and placed her hand over Ron's. "I know. They're pretty caught up in their work."

"Understatement much?" Ron shrugged. "I know they love me, but they aren't the most engaged parents. Forget about them; they just give me more space to create. Tell me more about your switch."

Tina squirmed with happiness. "I'm dropping biology and switching to applied mathematics."

Ron frowned. "Why would your mom be worried about that?"

Tina raised an eyebrow. "That's not all. I'm taking modules in interpersonal management, too."

Ron laughed. "Oh, I see where you're going with this. Two tracks? Yeah, your mom is going to be worried about you burning yourself out."

"Which is why I need to practice my argument for when I tell her. I'm not going to see much of anyone for the next couple of years."

Ron did a double take. "You'll still have time for me, right?"

Tina shrugged. "Realistically, I can't see how. I'm barely going to have time to sleep. Anyway, you're starting with Jean's team. You won't have time to see me, either." She let go of his hand and sat back against the shiny leather seat. "You *have* realized that we need to take a break while we get our careers off the ground, right?"

"No?" he spluttered. "I mean... A break?"

Tina saw time stop for Ron. His face fell even as it reddened, and his eyes began to shine. "Ron, it isn't forever. It's just a break."

Ron frowned. "It's *not* just a break. It's a break-*up*, out of nowhere. I did not see it coming."

Tina made a face. "You hadn't considered where you were going to fit in time to maintain a healthy relationship with me? Ron, your work will be just as time-consuming as my studies! You won't have any more time for me than I'll have for you. Honestly, it's like you forget logic exists sometimes."

"There you go again with the snark!"

Tina shrugged at Ron's sulky response. "If you hate my snarkiness that much, then a break won't be a problem, will it?" She held up her hands. "Look, I'm not saying we'll never see each other, but our energy needs to go into building the future so we have a future to enjoy–*when* we get there. If my parents' relationship has taught me anything, it's that I won't settle for anything less than healthy. I watched how hard my mom worked to rebuild herself from the ground up after John saved us from my asshole dad. I won't *ever* go through that."

She could tell Ron wasn't even listening, and she waved a hand in front of his face. "Ron, did you hear me?"

Ron glared at the ice cream puddle in the bottom of the bowl, stirring it angrily. "I heard you, but I don't get why you're doing this. I'm nothing like your dad."

Tina dropped her head onto the table and groaned with exasperation. Her arms muffled her voice. "I didn't say you were!"

Ron said nothing.

When she looked up, the opposite side of the booth was empty and Ron was on the other side of the diner pulling the door open angrily.

Tina considered calling him back for half a second, but her pride stung as much as the frustrated tears in her eyes. *Why doesn't he listen? I wish he'd actually* listen *instead of just hearing what he thinks I'm saying. Ugh!*

She got up and left by the opposite door.

CHAPTER FIVE

Q BBS *Meredith Reynolds*, All Guns Blazing

Marcus hummed to himself as he left the bar.

He paused at the service corridor when he heard a sniffle and sidetracked to investigate. He poked his head into the corridor and saw Tina sitting hunched over her knees, sobbing with her face in her hands.

He almost tripped over his feet in his hurry to get to her. "Tina, what's wrong? Are you hurt?"

Tina looked up, utterly miserable. "It's Ron! He's such a *jerk* sometimes!"

Marcus took a step back, flummoxed. An injury to her body he knew how to deal with, but a broken heart?

Tina gave a choking laugh at his distress. "It's okay, Marcus. I'm fine, really. We just had a fight, is all." She scrubbed her raw cheeks with damp sleeves.

Marcus didn't miss the clues; she'd been here a while. Still, what to do?

He knelt next to her and awkwardly patted her on the shoulder. "Cheer up, Tina. It's not like you're going to see much of him after graduation. You're young. You'll find a new crush soon. Plenty more fish in the sea and all that…" His voice trailed off as Tina burst into fresh tears.

Oh, dear. "I'm sorry, that was the wrong thing to say. Matters of the heart are not my strong point."

Tina made a face. "You don't say. I said I'll be fine, Marcus."

Marcus shook his head. "Well, you don't look fine to me. Come on, let's get you to the office. I think we have a few Cokes left in the fridge, and you can tell me and the guys all about it."

He held out a hand to pull her up and steered her out of the corridor and over to the private entrance to BMW's offices.

"You don't have to look after me, Marcus," she protested as the door swung shut behind them. "I would have been okay."

It was Marcus' turn to make a face. "If that's true, why were you camped out right where I would find you? I'm glad you're here, actually. I had a favor to ask you."

Tina shrugged and let him lead her into the main work-room. She loved the smell of the offices: a combination of musty paper, engine grease, man-sweat, and stale beer. It was homey and messy, and she loved being there.

Bobcat and William were hard at work, which meant they were drinking and slinging insults over a messy workstation.

William banged his fist on the table. "I'm telling you, it will have to do."

"And I'm telling *you* that those tolerances aren't accept-able!" Bobcat bellowed, looking at the spilled beer on the table with pure horror. "Bethany Anne wants this done *yesterday*. And you spilled my beer!"

Tina's spirits lifted at the familiar banter and she giggled, distracting Bobcat and William from their debate.

Bobcat grinned at her. "Heya, Tina! Nice to see you." He saw her puffy eyes. "What's wrong, sweetheart?"

"Boy trouble," Marcus told him, oblivious to Tina's rapidly reddening face. "I'll go and get you that Coke, Tina." He left the room, heading for the fridge they kept to cut down on beer runs while they were working.

Tina sat down across from Bobcat and William. "I had a fight with Ron," she admitted in answer to their searching expressions. "He doesn't get that things are going to change after graduation. And I'm *Gott Verdammt* sick of him saying I'm too snarky! I'm a snarky person! It's not *my* fault he's not sharp enough to keep up."

"There's no such thing as *too* snarky, sweetheart." William shook his head in disappointment. "Pay him no mind. Young Ronnie obviously hasn't learned that females are the superior sex yet."

Bobcat winked and pounded his fist into his free hand a few times. "Want us to go and fix his wagon?"

Hanging out with BMW was always a sure-fire way to shift a bad mood. Tina shook her head and bent over the table to look at the scattered plans, all misery forgotten. "No, it's okay. I feel better now. What are you guys working on?"

Bobcat moved the empties as she spread the sheets out. "It's Reynolds' project. You probably shouldn't be…"

Tina ignored him and her eyes lit up as she flipped through the plans. "A death ray? *Cool…*" A small furrow formed between her eyes as she fell into the calculations. She snatched Bobcat's pencil and began adjusting numbers here and there. "Your math is a little off. The beer can rings are really distracting, you know. Here," she made a final squiggle, "that should help."

She was about to reach for the next stack of papers when she was distracted by a high-pitched squeak.

"I think you could help with this little one if you wanted to?" Marcus asked, holding out the squirming ball of fur responsible for the noise she'd heard. "She needs a name and someone to look after her until we can find her a forever home."

Tina almost squealed with joy. "A kitten! Oh, Marcus, she's so sweet!" She held out her hands to take the kitten from him gently. "What's your name?" she asked the kitten, holding it up so she could see. "Maybe Tiger, for your stripes?"

The kitten objected to the height, digging needle-like claws into Tina's hands. "*Ow! Fu...*" she remembered where she was, "...dge." She turned bright red as the guys looked at her, unable to believe their ears. "Hey, you can't blame me! You guys curse all the time. It was bound to rub off eventually. Drunken pottymouths, all three of you!"

"Hey! I resemble that remark!" Bobcat complained.

"That's my defense, and I'm sticking to it!" Tina grinned, snuggling the kitten.

Marcus chuckled. "Looks like we have a name for the fluffball. Fudge it is!"

Tina held Fudge to her chest, inhaling the kitten-smell happily. "Can I really take her with me?" Fudge began to knead her with her tiny paws.

Marcus beamed. "Of course you can. That's why I gave her to you, Tina. However, you'll have to take good care of her until we find her a home. If she's too much to take care of, bring her back, okay?"

"Okay," Tina agreed. She hugged him with her free arm and danced out of the office, cradling Fudge carefully. "Thanks, guys!"

Marcus looked at the changes Tina had made to the calculations. "By God, she fixed it!"

Bobcat and William gaped as Marcus showed them the corrections.

"How did we miss that?" Bobcat moaned.

William thumped him on the arm. "Too busy thinking about beer, that's how!"

Bobcat looked pained. "It's like you know me or something!" He shook his head and looked at Marcus. "That girl is going to put us three on the scrapheap when she grows up."

"You can't say the Ds didn't warn us," Marcus agreed. "Still, I'm glad I could do something to cheer her up."

William looked up from the table. "Hey, Marcus, here's something you didn't think about. Tina is back at school now, right? Did you ask the Ds if Tina could look after that cat?"

Marcus paled. "Um…"

CHAPTER SIX

Q BBS *Meredith Reynolds*, **Etheric Academy, Main Lobby, One Week Later**

Devi paused at the doors to the administrative wing and sniffed delicately.

She liked the human children, but she'd learned to take a minute or two for her sensitive nose to adjust to the heady mixture of the scents they sprayed on themselves, not to mention the hormones the adolescents exuded when they encountered each other.

She greeted the students with happy chuffs as she made her morning rounds before class. *They might smell funny, but they always bring me a treat...or three. Who am I to disappoint them by refusing?*

On the first day Dorene had accompanied Devi to ensure that the students did not mob her, but all had been respectful of her space–especially after Dorene had made it clear that anyone harassing her would be in a world of trouble. Since then, Devi had made her rounds each morning and then sat in on whichever classes took her interest that day.

Today she was excited; she was going to see a rabbit for the first time!

The name alone intrigued her. She felt like they were something she needed to know about. The still images Ms. Treble had shown the class had stirred her, speaking to her puppy heart of a canine glory she had yet to experience.

Her parents had just looked at each other and burst into doggy laughter when she'd told them about the rabbits.

She wondered what they looked like when they ran...

She trotted up the stairs leading to the classrooms, puffing out her chest so her sparkly tie caught the light of the galaxy display and making sure her tail was fluffed out for maximum prettiness as she went. She caught up with Mischa and Masha at the top, her tail starting to wag the moment she saw her friends. The device on her collar translated her chuffs of greeting for the twins. "Mischa, Masha! Today is the day we see the rabbits!"

The twins smiled at her, something she'd had to get used to with humans. The wolf-natured didn't see that human expression as a threat, bared teeth or no, so Devi had learned not to either. She wagged her tail harder.

As always, Mischa and Masha bent down to Devi's eye-level and began fishing around in their pockets for a treat. That was one of the reasons she loved the twins—they always had a bit of jerky on them. "Yes, Devi. Did you ask Meredith to show you the vids?"

Devi shook her head. "Seeing is overrated. I want to *smell* the rabbits. Vids can't do that."

The twins nodded and did the strange shoulder movement Devi could never manage to duplicate.

"We'd better get into the classroom before Ms. Treble gets here."

Devi liked how Mischa and Masha did things at the same time. They reminded her of her bonded humans, only the girls were much more liberal with the treats than Diane and Dorene. *They* only gave her the treats she'd earned, which she respected.

Still, free jerky was free jerky.

She followed Masha and Mischa into the classroom and hopped onto one of the seats made for four-legged Yollins as usual. She stretched out on the padded cushion and listened to the twins talk with Yana about the trip. There weren't any Yollins at the Academy just yet, but they would be well provided for when they arrived.

In the meantime, they make good puppy chairs. Devi made herself comfortable on the cushion while they waited for the teacher.

Ms. Treble breezed through the door a few minutes later. "Good morning, class! I hope you're all ready to visit with Boomer and his family?"

Devi jumped to attention with a happy yip, her tail wagging hard enough to create a breeze.

Her excitement was to be short-lived.

Ms. Treble checked attendance before leading the students down to where Max was waiting to take them to the plants and ecologies area.

"Morning, kids," he called from the driver's compartment. "Morning, Devi. Dorene told me you were excited to see the rabbits today."

"You bet I am!" Devi yipped, her tie flapping as she spun in a circle.

"We'll be there soon. Settle down now, Devi," Ms. Treble told her. "You can look out of the window and tell us when you see the cornfield."

Devi jumped onto the seat next to Masha and put her paws on the window. "Yes, ma'am."

Ms. Treble went to the driver's compartment to speak with Max.

"I like her," Yana declared. "All that stuff in class about which fly had whatever-colored eyes should have been awful to sit through, but she made it interesting."

"Yeah," Halli agreed. "Her name is pretty, too. I have a cousin named Katie."

Yana leaned over to get a closer look at Devi's paws. "Is that nail polish?"

"It's my pet-icure," Devi chuffed. "Mischa did it."

"It's very pretty, Devi. We should have a girls' night soon, I bet the polish doesn't last long with you walking around all day."

Mischa grinned. "You'd be surprised. Ron made it just for Devi. It's made of a similar material to the stuff they paint the antigrav shipping containers with. Nothing will chip it. Ron gave me a special remover with the polish."

"That's...amazing," Yana breathed. "It *never* chips?"

Mischa shook her head.

Halli's eyes shone. "Not even if I was working on an engine? Wow, that *is* amazing."

Katie returned from the driver's compartment as the tram pulled to a halt. "We're here, class. Gather your belongings and join me at the door." She smiled at her students, thinking about how she'd ended up here.

Leaving Earth behind for the Queen's benevolent dictatorship, embarking on this crazy adventure? It was the best decision she'd ever made.

She'd spent her twenties teaching science in the most challenging public schools, her initial hopeful wide-eyed naïveté turning to shock, dismay, and eventually downright fury at what the education system offered children in the inner cities. The children in these areas had no chance of a brighter tomorrow when their schools were underfunded, understaffed, and outmoded—not to mention unsafe.

Her colleagues all had the same tired, jaded attitude, but Katie had never been the type of woman to back down from a challenge, so she had done whatever she could. She'd bought books and school supplies for students out of her wages, even bringing food for kids who arrived at school with empty bellies on more occasions than she could remember.

She organized after-school clubs, community projects, and cultural experiences on top of her teaching duties, all in the hope of opening their young eyes to the possibilities in the world.

It hadn't been enough to keep the majority of her students from failing to launch after high school, but the few she had helped to realize their potential had never forgotten her.

Katie had waged war against a broken system, resigning

from teaching to tackle the root of the issues directly in her early thirties. Her singular focus was tearing it up from the inside and becoming a thorn in the side of the bureaucrats. She was present at every meeting, every gala, fête, or fundraiser, campaigning relentlessly for equal provision for those below the poverty line.

She fought until she could fight no more. The doctors back on Earth had given her months to live at most—then TQB and Bethany Anne had turned everything on its head. Katie had been invited to the *Polaris*, and her death sentence had been repealed. She had sworn to serve Bethany Anne in whatever capacity she was needed.

She just hadn't expected the call back to teaching.

When Dorene had approached her about taking a position at the Academy she'd initially turned it down, unable to face another go-round of seeing bright minds crushed by a system designed to slot them into preconceived boxes or be left behind.

The Velasquez sisters' retraining program had quickly disabused her of that notion. The children of the Etheric Academy were to be taught differently, each given the freedom to find their own path, their own inspiration. Her job as a teacher was to guide them as they grew to their full potential, *not* to strip them of their individuality and force them into some preconceived mold to meet an arbitrary target. None of *them* would be left behind.

Katie had fallen in love with teaching again.

The tram's doors opened and the class disembarked under her direction. It was a short walk from there past the fields to the animal habitats. Katie spotted another German

Shepherd puppy playing fetch with a four-legged Yollin at the edge of the cornfield.

Huh, the things you see.

They were met at the entrance to the rabbit habitat by a thickset woman in her mid-fifties wearing a sweater set and a scowl.

"That dog is not welcome here," the woman complained as a greeting, pointing an accusatory finger at Devi. "It'll scare my rabbits."

Katie was taken aback. "You didn't say anything when we spoke, Bernadette. I sent you the student roster. Besides, Devi is an enhanced dog. She would never do anything to scare the rabbits."

Devi wagged her tail and chuffed. "I'm here to *learn* about the rabbits, Ms. Treble."

Katie smiled at the puppy. "I know you are, precious." She had a soft spot for all animals, and Devi was a delight to her. She stood and faced the woman. "Bernadette, be reasonable."

Bernadette's scowl deepened, and she folded her arms tightly as she glared at the puppy. "Either the dog leaves or you all do."

Katie narrowed her eyes, trying to work out the woman's issue. "I don't understand. The class is scheduled; you can't cancel it."

Bernadette's chin jutted as she spoke. "No. Dogs. Take it up with whomsoever you like, but the dog stays outside."

Devi whined, looking up at the woman in confusion.

Katie bent down and reassured Devi with a gentle hand on her neck. "I'm so sorry, Devi, but we're on a schedule today. I saw one of your littermates over by the cornfield. Perhaps you'd like to go and join them for now? I promise I'll deal with this later, but for now we need to get class underway."

"Okay," Devi chuffed. She looked up at Bernadette. "I'm telling my humans about you. You're *mean*!" She stalked toward the cornfield with her tail held high and a dignified tilt to her snout.

Ms. Treble addressed the students. "Go on in, class. I need a quick word with Bernadette and I'll be right along." She watched them file into the building before turning a stern look on the woman. "This is entirely unacceptable, Bernadette. Devi has as much right to learn without discrimination as any of the other students. What if I had brought a Yollin? Would you turn them away, too?"

The rabbit handler blanched. "How *dare* you, Katie! Wait until I speak to the Academy administrators!" She turned on her heel and marched inside.

Katie turned to check on Devi one last time before she went inside; she and the white puppy she'd seen earlier were tussling at the side of the field.

She snickered as she closed the door behind herself. She had a class to teach, and she was happy to let Bernadette run to Diane and Dorene. When she got back to her office, she would make popcorn and watch the verbal flaying the wretched woman got when the Velasquez twins found out their puppy had been treated so poorly.

CHAPTER SEVEN

Q BBS *Meredith Reynolds*, **Medical Level**

Masha and Mischa skirted a commotion as they passed through the lobby after school ended. Masha glanced with concern at the three orderlies restraining a distressed man in a hospital gown who was trying to leave, but Mischa was so busy talking she barely even noticed the two Guardians appear from the west corridor.

"I felt sorry for Devi. She really wanted to see the rabbits," Mischa prattled, oblivious to the drama. "Poor puppy. Bernadette should have told me she wouldn't be allowed in the building before we arrived. Did you see how sad she was when she had to wait outside?"

"At least Snow was there to keep her company," Masha offered.

Mischa nodded. "I suppose so. I cannot believe Craig is in Medical *again*. I really thought he would stop doing stupid things now that he's a Guardian."

Masha snorted. "I can believe it. It's been a while since

51

he took that epic beat-down by the Chinese Guardian team. You didn't think our foolish wolf would go too long without another mishap, did you?"

Mischa and Masha strolled down the corridor to the ward where Craig was recovering from yet another injury.

"Maybe all those darts screwed with his brain." Masha snickered, twirling a finger next to her temple. "I know *I* wouldn't have asked Jian for a rematch. Have you *seen* the vid from when the three of them took Craig down?"

Mischa's cheeks turned pink. "Well, *I* thought it was brave of him—if a little stupid—but that's Craig all over. He wouldn't be Craig if he didn't put his heart into everything he does."

They took the turn onto the ward, waving to the nurses as they passed the station by the door.

"Have you gone sweet on him?" Masha's eyes narrowed, scrutinizing her twin's face as she held the door. "You *have*!"

Mischa's blush deepened. "Shut up, Masha!" she hissed. "He'll hear you!"

Craig had a twinkle in his eye when they entered his room but whether he'd heard them or was just in pain Mischa couldn't tell. Either way, his face was pretty much the only thing they could see that wasn't covered by a plaster cast or the blanket strategically draped over him.

Mischa gasped when she saw the traction apparatus. "Craig, how bad is it?"

Masha was close beside her sister. "Yeah, dude, what happened?"

"You haven't seen the vid?" They shook their heads.

Craig groaned. "I suppose you're gonna see it eventually. Meredith, put the video of my fight with Jian on, please."

"Of course, Craig." Meredith's voice held the edge of a laugh. The TV on the wall came on and the video began to play.

"Who's the leopard?" Masha asked. "I thought you said you fought Jian?"

"That *is* Jian," Craig told them.

The twins watched the screen as a wolf–Craig–and the leopard who was Jian charged at each other from opposite ends of the room.

Masha made a face of appreciation as Jian pulled a sweet maneuver which sent Craig flying into the wall at high speed, leaving a huge dent when he hit. Mischa gasped as onscreen Craig slid down into a crumpled heap on the mat below with his spine twisted at an unnatural angle.

"What, no snark from my favorite sisters?" Craig blew upwards to dislodge a tuft of hair from his eyes. "It's not as bad as it looks. I'm getting out of here in a few days. Do me a solid and move that hair out of my face, will you? It's been driving me crazy."

Masha looked at Craig's chart and tried to make sense of the indecipherable squiggles on it. "Dude, that looked painful."

Craig twitched, as much movement as the apparatus would allow him to make. "Yeah, wasn't expecting him to be a cat, to be honest. Why didn't anyone tell me? That's what I want to know."

Masha chuckled dryly. "A better question to ask is why you didn't bother to find out what he was capable of before you challenged him." She waved the chart at him. "Twenty-seven separate injuries to your spine? Wouldn't it have been easier to think before you acted?"

"I can feel every one of them. And you don't need to tell me; I've heard it all from Commander Silvers." Craig tried not to wince. "It wouldn't have been so serious, but I hit the part of the wall covering the support beam. Snapped me like a dry twig."

Mischa tucked the stray hair back into the cast. "Oh, you poor thing! Are your nanos not healing the damage?"

Craig winced. "They are, but I have to stay totally still until my spine heals."

Masha wrinkled her nose. "It won't take more than a day or two. Why haven't you been healed in the Pod-doc?"

"Commander Silvers decided I still hadn't learned my lesson, so traction it is. He said it would 'give me time to consider,' or something."

Yana and Bai Hu came in, and Tina joined them all a moment later with a Tupperware container in one hand and a squirming ball of fluff in the other. She put the container on Craig's over-bed table. "Hey, my mom sent this to help you heal faster. It's still warm." She put the kitten down on the table and cracked the lid of the tub, letting out a rich meaty aroma.

Craig moaned. "If only I could sit up to eat it! Where's Ron and Aleksei?"

Tina shut the lid before the kitten could dip her tiny paw into the gravy. "Fudge, that's *not* for you!" Fudge left the tub to pounce at a shadow cast by Craig's traction apparatus. "They're deep into a project, and I haven't seen Ron since he decided to be a sulky baby. He did leave me a gift; a kitty-cam so I can check in while Fudge is alone in the dorm. But if he thinks *that's* enough to get him out of the doghouse, he's got another think coming."

"Don't hold back there, Tina," Craig joked. "Tell us how you *really* feel!"

She stuck her tongue out at him. "I can always keep the brisket."

"No–*ow*!"

Bai Hu stared at the apparatus holding Craig in place. "Does it hurt?"

Craig tried to shake his head. "Only when I try to move. Oh, man, it's a good thing I have this holding me still."

"What happened to you?" Yana asked, tickling Fudge's dappled tummy with a finger. "Halli didn't really say."

Craig reddened. "I hit a wall at the wrong angle."

Masha snickered. "He asked Jian for a rematch and lost."

"Hey!" Craig protested. "I *almost* had him."

Everyone snickered at that. Fudge hissed, suddenly catching the scent of Bai Hu.

"It's okay, Fudge," Tina told her kitten. "Bai Hu is nice."

Fudge didn't appear to agree. She skittered up Tina's arm and over her shoulder, tucking herself under Tina's hair where she could keep an eye on the human-who-smelled-like-a-cat.

There was a soft knock at the door and a nurse walked in. "I thought you already had somebody in here. You've got a lot of visitors today, Craig." She smiled at them all. "Just don't tire him out, okay?"

"We won't," Yana promised.

The nurse left and a Chinese man wearing a Guardian uniform came in.

"Jian!" Craig couldn't hide his surprise. "You haven't come to finish me off, have you? At least wait until I get out of traction!"

Jian chuckled as he crossed the room.

When Bai Hu saw Jian's uniform he panicked. Quicker than the eye could see, the sweet little boy was gone and in his place was an angry juvenile white tiger standing atop a puddle of activewear. Bai Hu jumped between Yana and Jian, hissing and spitting as he swiped the air between them with splayed claws.

Tina shrieked as Fudge lost her tiny kitten mind at the sight of the tiger and clawed her way out of Tina's hair, scrambling upward. "*Fudge!*" Tina just missed catching the kitten as she made a leap of faith from the top of Tina's head and landed on Craig's crotch.

"ARGH!"

Tina rushed to grab the kitten, who was scrabbling for purchase on the blanket as Craig cried out in pain.

"Bai Hu!" Yana scolded. "Change back! It's just Jian. He is not our enemy. I'm so sorry, Jian. He must associate you with the soldiers who hunted him before we found him."

Jian shook his head as if the reason didn't matter and exuded calm as he waited for Bai Hu to realize he was no threat to Yana. Bai Hu yowled to warn the Guardian to stay back, but Jian didn't back off—and he didn't attack either. He sat down on the floor with his legs crossed, arms resting loosely in his lap and a patient smile on his face.

Bai Hu's ears went back and his tail swished in confusion. He backed up and sat back on his haunches in front of Yana, never breaking eye contact with Jian or ceasing his snarl.

"What's going on?" Craig cried, interested now that there wasn't a kitten clawing at his groin.

Jian's voice was calm and slow. "It is nothing to worry about. The little cat is afraid of me." He didn't take his eyes from the tiger in front of him. "Your name is Bai Hu? I had a friend named Bai once. He was brave, just like you. I mean you no harm, *xiǎo māo*. In fact, I am just like you. Can you smell my cat?"

The tiger's mouth opened as he tasted the air, his sensitive Jacobson's organ picking out the Were element of Jian's scent. Yana held up a sheet for Bai Hu when he changed back to his human form a second later.

The young werecat stared at his elder for a long moment. "I thought all my people were gone, that I was the only cat here. You are not a tiger. Are you a soldier?"

Jian gave a slight shake of his head as he got up in one fluid movement. "I used to be. Now I am a Guardian and I serve the Queen. I am a leopard when I change."

"Why did you not change when I changed?"

Jian smiled gently, patting Bai Hu on the shoulder. "I did not come here today to attack a frightened child." He took the few steps to Craig's bed. "I am stationed on the medical level tonight. I came to make sure I had not permanently injured you on my way to my post."

Craig groaned. "This traction is a pain in the ass, or should I say, an itch I can't scratch, but I'll be healed soon. Dude, you know I can't leave it like this, don't you?"

Jian lowered his head fractionally. "I would expect

nothing less from someone of your…enthusiasm. I look forward to schooling you in patience once again."

Craig laughed, then groaned again with pain as the movement wracked his ribs. "Screw you, Hotdog Man. I'm gonna be ready for you and your Zen-ness next time."

That elicited a dry twitch of the lips from Jian. "I will believe it when I see it. My 'Zen-ness,' as you call it, will not continue to extend to you if you keep calling me 'Hotdog Man.'" He looked down at Bai Hu. "Would you care to take a walk, young Bai? I believe we have much to talk about."

Bai Hu looked eagerly at Yana for permission.

Yana hugged him. "Go ahead, *Kotenok*. But get dressed first, yes? I will see you back at the Academy later."

A grinning Bai Hu skipped out after Jian. Yana watched them leave with a concerned expression.

"He'll be okay, right?"

"Who, Bai Hu?" Craig grinned. "Sure. Jian is cool."

"Why'd you call him 'Hotdog Man?'"

Craig snickered. "You know, because he's One with everything…"

Jian spoke in Mandarin, putting Bai Hu at ease. "You were very brave in there. It takes a lot of courage to put yourself between that which you fear and those you love."

Bai Hu walked alongside Jian, studying the older were-cat's serene face. "Yana is my sister," he declared fiercely. "I would stand between her and *any* danger. You are the one who hurt Craig."

Jian shook his head. "Craig was injured because he did not make the effort to find out about my enhancement. Know your opponent, Bai Hu. It is a hard lesson well learned that will keep Craig alive later in life."

Bai Hu did not agree, but he kept his opinion to himself. "Where are we going?"

Jian pointed to the elevator ahead of them. "I like to walk through the cornfields now and then. So...'Bai Hu.'" Jian chuckled. "You are very well named. I've seen many Sacred Clan tigers, but never a white one."

"My family was not a part of the Sacred Clan. We hid from them like we hid from the government until they found us and sent the soldiers." Bai Hu hung his head. "I killed many soldiers in my tiger form. Even though it was in my family's defense, I do not want to kill any more people. There must be another way."

"I did not expect to become a cat," Jian told him softly, pressing the call button for the elevator. "My life on Earth was spent at war with the Sacred Clan, and they killed my dear friend Bai. But accepting my heritage was easy when we battled the Yollins, and I see more of the same ahead. It is my duty to protect my friends, and in this my feelings about the Sacred Clan do not matter. The only thing that matters is that by going into the Pod-doc I have become strong enough to protect them from harm. It was not a decision I made lightly, but it was the right one. You will find your path, Bai Hu. You are free to choose what fulfills you, but if you do not accept who you are the path will be difficult to see."

They rode the elevator in silence, Bai Hu contemplating Jian's words. He didn't like being so scared when his tiger broke free that he put everyone around him in danger when he lost control. He was sure that other eleven-year-olds did not have to contemplate a future filled with death and destruction. His experiences of both of those things before he had been brought to the *Meredith Reynolds* had been enough to last him a lifetime.

What made him happy was being at home with the family who loved him enough to take him into their hearts. He loved his school, and even more, he loved visiting Yana at the Academy so he could examine the ever-expanding galaxy projection in the lobby.

"I do not wish to be the cause of anyone's death. All I want is to be with my family and study the stars."

Jian smiled as the elevator doors opened. "I think there will be plenty of room for an astronomer on the journey ahead."

QBBS *Meredith Reynolds*, Etheric Academy, Alpha Class Dormitory

Back from the medical wing, Tina shut the door and put Fudge down on the floor carefully.

The kitten purred and rubbed her face on Tina's leg before sauntering off to inspect her food bowl.

"Are you hungry, Fudge?" She picked up the bowl on the way to the kitchen area and filled it with kitty kibble. Fudge continued purring, making little hops with her front paws as she twined herself around Tina's legs. "There you go, sweet girl." She poured a mug of milk, put it in the microwave for hot chocolate, and replaced Fudge's water while it warmed.

The door opened and Ron and Aleksei came in, arms loaded with electronic components.

"Watch out for Fudge!" Tina hurried over and scooped up the surprised kitten quickly before she made a dash for the open door. The administrators had been clear that she would only be allowed to have Fudge at the Academy if she kept her in the dorm.

Ron placed his load on the table next to Aleksei's and reached out awkwardly to stroke the kitten, who hissed at him and clung to Tina. "Was she okay while you were in class today?"

Tina nodded grudgingly, nuzzling Fudge's nose with her own. Fudge blinked and batted at Tina's hair. "The kitty-cam was a good idea. I came back and fed her at lunch, and she slept from then until I picked her up on the way to visit Craig. I had to bring her back early because Bai Hu went all tiger and scared her. The twins will be here soon. They stopped by to see Devi."

"If I was the size of a mouthful I would be afraid of a tiger too!" Aleksei joked. "She's going to have the zoomies tonight. I am glad I will be fast asleep in my dorm!"

Tina narrowed her eyes at Aleksei as she replaced Fudge on the floor.

Ron interjected. "Knock it off, Aleksei. Tina, we made progress on our project today."

Tina's face lit up. "That's great!" She laughed at the confusion her abrupt change of mood caused both boys.

"There's still a ways to go, but once we're done we'll be able to feel the wind on our faces again!" Ron replied, tentatively accepting Tina's olive branch—however temporary. "How was Craig?"

Tina was just about to tell them about Craig when a commotion at the door distracted them.

Masha and Mischa came in with Devi. The twins were consoling the puppy, who was still indignant about not being allowed inside the rabbit habitat.

"It isn't fair," Devi complained, her translation device giving the words a pouty tone. "I want to see the— What is that *smell?*" Her whining ceased and her ears pricked up as she zeroed in on the kitten, who was at that moment sharpening her claws on the sofa.

"Intruder!" Devi growled, ready to pounce.

Fudge jumped into the air and spun to face Devi, and the animals stared at each other, hackles up.

Tina cried out in alarm, "Devi, *NO!* You leave Fudge alone!"

The twins rushed to hold Devi back, but there was no need.

The tiger was still fresh in Fudge's mind. She had seen scarier things than an overgrown puppy that day.

Fudge's stripy fur stood on end, making her appear twice as big as usual. She hissed at Devi and batted the German Shepherd's nose with her tiny claws extended.

"Owww!" Devi yelped and jumped back. She pressed a paw to her nose. "What kind of evil creature is that?"

Fudge sat down, nonchalantly washing her ears with the air of one confident of her place in the pecking order.

"Serves you right for scaring a helpless kitten," Masha told Devi. She held out her arms for the puppy. "Here, let me see."

"Helpless? Look what the monster did to me! I'm

ALPHA CLASS 04: GRADUATION

wounded!" Devi whined, holding her stinging snout in the air for Masha's inspection.

Tina passed Masha a damp cloth to use to dab at Devi's snout. "There you go. You're not bleeding. Fudge isn't an intruder, Devi. I'm looking after her for Marcus, and that means you have to look after her, too. Don't scare her."

Devi huffed, eyeing the kitten suspiciously. "If you say so, but she *smells* like an enemy and my nose has never lied to me. I'll look after her, but only so I'm there to protect you when she turns traitor."

Fudge gave Devi a look of pure feline disdain, then got up and stalked toward the sleeping area with her tail held straight in the air. When she got to the door, the kitten glanced back and fixed Devi with a cool look before sauntering off.

"See?" The puppy was indignant. "She's evil. Evil, I tell you!" Devi looked around at the humans. "Why are you laughing? She'll be the end of us all!"

CHAPTER EIGHT

Q BBS *Meredith Reynolds*, **All Guns Blazing, BMW Offices**

Tina stood at the door to the office holding her tablet in one hand and Fudge's kitty carrier in the other. "Meredith, would you let me in, please?"

"Shouldn't you be at the Academy, Tina?"

Tina could have sworn she heard a hint of disapproval in Meredith's usually equable tone. "I haven't snuck out, if that's what you're implying," she told the EI indignantly. "I got a pass; you can check. Marcus is expecting me."

"Very well."

"Thank you, Meredith."

The door opened and Tina wandered through the offices until she found Marcus sitting at his computer. She cleared the empty beer cans that Bobcat had left away, sweeping them off the table into the trashcan with a tinny crash, and put Fudge's carrier down next to the scientist.

He looked up from his screen, startled. "Oh! Oh, it's just you, Tina. I wasn't expecting you until this afternoon."

TS PAUL

Tina took in his red-rimmed eyes, two-day stubble, and the grubbiness of his clothing. "Marcus, it *is* afternoon! In fact, it's later than that. Have you worked right around the clock again?"

Marcus grinned sheepishly, rubbing a hand over his stubble. "Huh, I guess I have. How's the kitten?"

Tina opened the top zipper on the carrier and Fudge hopped out, much to Marcus' surprise. "She's doing great, unlike you."

Marcus wiggled a finger for Fudge to bat at, ignoring Tina's snark. "So, what did you want to see me about?"

Tina shook her finger at him, putting the other hand on her hip. "Oh, no! You don't get away with it that easily, Marcus Cambridge!"

Marcus' brow furrowed. "Get away with what?"

"Not looking after yourself! Go take a shower and change your stinky clothes and *then* I'll tell you what I came here for." She raised an eyebrow and pointed at the door, giving Marcus no choice but to obey.

He sighed. "I know when I'm defeated." As he got up to leave he glanced at the indefatigable seventeen-year-old. "You are a very bossy young woman."

Tina smirked, sitting down to give Fudge the attention she was demanding. "And *you* are a forgetful old genius who needs a kick in the butt now and again. Now *go*. I missed lunch, so I don't want to miss dinner as well."

Marcus grinned as he headed for the door. "Who's forgetful now? You can just order something from the bar. Someone will bring it through."

Tina messaged her mom to say she was having dinner with Marcus, then ordered for the two of them before

66

setting out Fudge's food and water bowls from her bag while she waited for Marcus to return.

Twenty minutes later he came back from the bathroom clean-shaven and freshly dressed, followed shortly by their food.

Tim 'Rocky' Kinley came in through the secure door to the bar bearing two delicious-smelling pizza boxes. "Who's hungry?"

"*Me!*" Tina rushed over to take the boxes from the burly bouncer. "Thanks, Tim!"

Marcus gave Tim a wave from the table as he left and took the box Tina held out to him. They ate, chatting about nothing and appreciating the meal as Fudge scampered around their feet, playing with a crumpled napkin.

Tina watched the kitten with a smile as she finished her third slice. "That's better."

Marcus put his crust down and wiped his hands on a napkin. "As you're so fond of telling me, brains need calories to produce genius. Now, what did you want to talk about?"

Tina frowned, wiping the grease from her fingers. "School. Or more accurately, what I should do after graduation."

Marcus pushed his box away and sat back. "I thought you were all set to go into biology?"

She shook her head. "I switched to applied mathematics."

"*That's* how you fixed the ESD ray calculations! You've been studying!"

Tina giggled. "Nope, I'm just better than you are at

67

reading your writing through three layers of beer rings. I've certainly had enough practice!"

"I'm just pulling your leg. Your ability with numbers is astounding." Marcus beamed. "That cannon rig was excellent, given what you had to work with. I saw Jean's vid of the siege. So you want to be an engineer?"

Tina laughed. "And spend my days covered in grease? Not for me, thanks. I'm more of a problem-solver. But then, I also think what my mom does is pretty epic. Project management on the scale she's doing it is an art form."

Marcus shrugged. "So what's the problem?"

Tina gaped at him. "I just *told* you! I have to decide and get back to Dorene about it soonest."

He considered her dilemma for a long minute, picking at his pizza crust. "Consider the skill base you need for the career you want to have, and which track will prepare you best. Either way, you should keep up with your math studies. You have a gift, my dear."

Tina winked at Marcus as she snagged the last slice of pizza from his box. "Oh, I intend to. How else am I going to take over your department when you're ready to be put out to pasture?"

Marcus was lost for words once again.

QBBS *Meredith Reynolds*, Etheric Academy, PET Annex

Maxim breathed through the next move of the kata Peter had him practicing.

He drew his breath in slowly as he set his stance, then pushed it out fast as he executed the strike and landed in position ready for the next step.

In...and *out*. In...and *out*, letting his breathing be his guide as he moved through each technique.

He bent his knees and twisted to wind up momentum for the final kick, leaping as he swept his foot up and around at shoulder height before landing lightly on the mat to face Peter and make his *rei*.

Peter gave Maxim a round of applause as he bowed. "That was great! Let's go again, but this time remember to give your hips an extra twist as you bend for that last kick. I want to see your foot reach my head height this time."

Maxim nodded, taking a swig from his water bottle before seating himself in a low crouch with his back held straight, ready to begin the pattern of movements again.

Peter gave him the nod. "When you're ready. How are you feeling about seeing Doc Dietrich today?"

Maxim shook his head. "I do not know. Ambivalent, I suppose?"

Peter smiled knowingly. "Talking about it will help, buddy. Trust me. Now, let me see you make that kick go over my head."

Maxim regulated his breathing once more, his attention back on controlling his body to get the maximum effect out of each movement. He was grateful that the focus required to execute each kick, block, and strike perfectly afforded his tired mind a break.

Just the thought of his impending therapy session was enough to bring his troubles to the forefront and the distraction caused him to miss a step.

Peter saw Maxim's attention slip, the misstep leaving him undefended on his left side. "Hold onto your focus," he told the younger man. "Take it from the top."

Maxim ground to a halt and began again, but it was Peter's turn to be distracted by somebody pinging him.

Peter frowned as he received the message. "Sorry, Maxim. I've gotta go,"

"Is everything okay?" Maxim asked.

Peter nodded, grabbing his bag and heading for the door. "A situation I've been keeping my eye on needs my attention. Nothing to worry about. You just keep practicing, kiddo."

Maxim made a face at being called 'kiddo' but prepared to start over as the door shut behind Peter. Almost as soon as he'd begun his tablet beeped, reminding him to go to his appointment.

"Already? Stupid counseling," he grumbled to himself as he threw his pads into his bag and set off for the medical wing.

An hour later, Maxim left Doctor Dietrich's office and made his way to the Grimes residence.

Cheryl Lynn opened the door with a big smile. "Hey, Maxim!"

"Hey, Ms. Grimes," Maxim replied. "Is Nestor still here with Todd?"

"He is. Come on in." Cheryl Lynn stood aside so Maxim could enter. "We were about to have dinner. You and Nestor are welcome to stay if you'd like?"

Maxim was tempted. Cheryl Lynn's leftovers were legendary among the Alpha Class students. Anytime Tina visited home and didn't bring anything back with her, she heard about it from the others. "It smells really good, Ms. Grimes, but I wouldn't want to impose on you."

Cheryl Lynn grinned as she escorted him to Todd's room. "Such lovely manners, just like Nestor! Lord knows I made enough, and Tina's doing something over with Marcus so she's not going to make it. You boys will be doing me a favor if you stay and eat with us."

Maxim blushed. "You're the best, Ms. Grimes."

"I'll call when dinner's ready. You boys have fun." Cheryl Lynn smiled and left for the kitchen.

Maxim went into Todd's room, disturbing the younger boys from their game. He waved for them to continue and sat down on a chair to watch them play.

They quickly fell back into the deep concentration the game required as they tried to outdo each other's aerial exploits. It left Maxim some time to think about his mandatory counseling session.

It hadn't been anything like he'd expected. He'd gone into Doctor Dietrich's room prepared for an inquisition about his *feelings*.

Instead, the doctor had introduced himself and then let Maxim guide the conversation. It had been awkward at first—Maxim being the stoic type at the best of times —but Doctor Dietrich had pointed to the bag by Maxim's feet and asked what combat styles Maxim was training in.

Before Maxim knew it, his hour was up and nobody had mentioned the 'f' word once.

He had promised to return in two days' time for another 'discussion,' as the doctor had called it. He didn't know if the talking would help him at all, but the doctor had shown him a couple of sweet jujitsu moves he wanted to follow up on.

It looked like the game was coming to its conclusion.

Maxim thought he saw the finish line in the distance on the screen and a moment later Cheryl Lynn called them for dinner, just as they crossed the line in a photo finish.

"One minute, Mom!" Todd called back as they waited for the results to load.

Todd jumped up and took a victory pose. "WHOOP!"

Maxim looked on quizzically while Todd pulled his tablet out and Nestor dropped his head into his hands with a groan.

Todd pointed his tablet's camera at Nestor and grinned. "Come on, bro, you've got to do it! You made *me* do it last time!"

"I am making much less fuss than you did," Nestor snarked, tilting his chin at a defiant angle as he spoke to the camera through gritted teeth. "Todd Grimes is the best pilot there ever was or will be. He leaves us mere mortals in his space dust. All hail Todd Grimes."

Maxim burst into laughter, throwing the pillows from Todd's bed at both their heads. "It's crap like this that makes everyone else think pilots are arrogant narcissists."

"Hey, I can't help it if everyone feels compelled to acknowledge my awesomeness," Todd bragged, flexing his biceps as he strutted to the door.

Nestor punched Maxim in the arm as he went past. "You say a word about this to the others and I will never speak to you again."

. . .

QBBS *Meredith Reynolds*, Medical Level, Psychiatric Wing, Ward G

Peter gave Rickie a fist-bump as he came through the door and got a quick rundown of the day's events from his fellow original Guardian before he headed to the reception desk to speak to the nurse there.

He was pleasantly surprised to find the sterile white walls of the hospital corridor replaced by the warm décor of the ward. The walls were painted in a deep, pinkish terracotta and pale olive, there was art on the walls, and bookcases and potted plants filled the spaces between the overstuffed chairs and sofas in the waiting area. Beyond the reception desk, a half-wall topped with glass separated the dayroom, which Peter could see was just as thoughtfully detailed.

A nurse at the desk noticed his observation and smiled "You like it?"

"Yeah, it's nice. A big change from the other wards," He couldn't see her name badge. "Um..."

"Lucy. When this place was being designed, the Queen asked us how we would have it done if we were in charge. We all said that the long-term patients should be made to feel like they're at home, so a home is what she had them build. What can I do for you, Commander Silvers?"

Peter waved a hand at her. "Peter's fine. I got a message from Meredith about the Wechselbalg man with the memory loss. He made another attempt to leave?"

Lucy nodded. "Yeah, earlier today. It's okay, we had Rickie here to help out. It was a good thing you did—assigning us a Guardian. The presence of other Wechselbalg seems to soothe the patient when he's awake."

"That's why I came…about Ilya. I wanted to get the info on the woman who brought him in, but Meredith couldn't give it to me. Something about patient confidentiality?"

"Why do you want to know?" Lucy asked.

Peter shrugged. "I dunno. I guess this guy's situation is getting to me. Wechselbalg aren't made to be alone. I want to do the right thing by him, and maybe if I find out what the woman who found him knows I might be able to find someone who knows him among the Wechselbalg. All I need to start is her name and address, if you have it."

Lucy scrunched her mouth as she deliberated, and finally she sighed and reached for a scrap of paper and a pen. "I'm not supposed to do this, but he's gotten to all of us. I want you to promise you'll do your best to find his people."

Peter took the piece of paper from her with a grin. "You're an angel, Lucy. And I *will* do my best, I promise."

CHAPTER NINE

Q BBS *Meredith Reynolds*, **Etheric Academy, Cafeteria**

Yana lifted her breakfast tray over the students' heads as she made her way to one of the smaller tables in the corner where Tina sat by herself.

Tina looked up as Yana stopped at the table. "Oh. Hey."

"Mind if I join you?" Yana sat down opposite her friend, not waiting for a reply. She glanced at the Alpha Class table, catching Halli's eye and giving a little shrug.

Halli rolled her eyes toward Ron, who sat next to her looking equally morose. "Why aren't you sitting with everyone else? Did you and Ron have another fight?"

Tina sighed and stabbed her oatmeal with her spoon. "I don't want to talk about it."

Yana patted Tina's free hand in sympathy. "Okay, but I'm here if you change your mind."

Tina put her spoon down. "It's just... We graduate in a few weeks, and *then* what? We have to face facts, but Ron doesn't want to admit we're going our separate ways."

"But you can still see each other!" Yana exclaimed.

"How?" Tina shook her head. "I'm going to be studying too hard over the next few years to even *think* about personal time. Why can't we just enjoy the time we have before we graduate instead of arguing about the inevitable?"

Yana tried to keep a straight face. "That's..." she trailed off, searching for something positive to say, "practical," she finished lamely.

Tina shrugged and picked up her spoon again. "I can't help being practical. You can go sit with Ron if you like. I don't mind."

Yana looked over at Ron again. "No, everyone else is sitting with him. He doesn't need me as well."

Masha came over to join them, planting her tray next to Tina's. "Will you two just make up already?"

"Masha!"

Masha was unrepentant. "What, Yana? Do you want to spend the last few weeks of school with their impending breakup hanging over our heads?"

Yana sighed, getting up. "No. Masha is right, Tina. You two have to stop arguing. Come on, let's go sit with the others."

Masha picked her tray up again and joined Yana. "Are you coming?"

Tina stood up and shook her head. "I don't think so. You two go. I'm going back to the dorm to feed Fudge before class."

Yana watched her go. "I hate that they're fighting."

"Me too," Masha agreed with a sigh. "Like we haven't got enough going on."

Yana studied Masha's face. "You're not happy either?"

Masha snorted. "What have I got to be happy about? A few hundred years of playing by the rules and following orders in the Guardians?"

Yana was confused. "I thought you were going to be a spy or something?"

"Yeah, but apparently 'that's not a viable career path.'" She huffed. "I felt like I contributed something vital at the castle, you know? What I did led to us saving the doc's family. It made me realize that I want to be more than the hammer. I want to be the scalpel. I want to walk the line and protect the Empire from the shadows." Masha gazed at nothing, lost in her dream. "I would make a *good* spy, going from planet to planet saving the day with exploits *so* incredible that people wouldn't believe they were real."

Yana shot Masha a sympathetic look as they took their seats at the table with the others. "How do you even *become* a spy? And who would you spy *on*?"

"Every new alien we meet, of course!" Masha grinned. "But like my mom and dad said, there's no way that's going to happen. It's either DipCorps or the Guardians–and there's *no* way I'm subjecting myself to a lifetime of standing around in a cocktail dress making small talk with a bunch of arrogant fashion-conscious diplomats!"

Yana snickered. "You? Smalltalk?"

"I know, right? Can you see me being all fancy-pants in an evening dress and heels?" Masha stuck her pinkie finger out as she took a pointedly delicate sip of her juice. "I'll leave all that to Mischa, thank you very much. She fits right in with the society types."

"Hey!" Mischa complained, pointing her fork at her

twin. "Actually, no, you're right. I had an interesting discussion with Dean Hauser about my options, and I do like the idea of socializing in the name of the Empire. How did your interview go, Yana?"

"It was very informative. I have a much clearer idea of what to expect when my internship starts."

Masha tilted her head as she ate, waving for Yana to go on.

"My role will be to learn about each new species as we come into contact with them to facilitate smooth communications. While you were all down in Wales, one of the things Tina's mom had us do was sit in on her classes while she learned about the different species we expect to encounter. I want to know how we are different—and if our commonalities can bring us together in peace instead of war. Like Human Resources, but on a galactic scale."

Masha nodded, finishing her mouthful of food. "You have high hopes, Yana."

"How can I have anything else?" Yana declared. "I am human, and to be human *is* to hope!" She scooped the last bite of her breakfast up. "Hurry up now or we'll be late for the rabbits."

QBBS *Meredith Reynolds*, Plants and Ecologies Space, Rabbit Habitat

Masha sat cross-legged on a blanket on the floor with Mischa, Yana, and Halli.

They each held a rabbit on a towel on their knees, gently tugging a slicker brush through their rabbit's wool one clump at a time.

Around them in loose circles the rest of the students did the same, each depositing the loosened wool in baskets given to them for that purpose while Bernadette spoke about the rabbits.

The head handler paced back and forth in her jodhpurs, her wellingtons squeaking with every step. "While the regular angora rabbit sheds its wool every ninety days or so, the genetics team has tweaked our angoras to make that cycle shorter to increase fiber yields. This, along with an adjustment to the genes that regulate the density of the angoras' wool, makes our angoras an ideal animal to fulfill our needs. While the Queen's dogs are fluffy and cute, they do nothing to help our self-sufficiency."

Yana frowned. "Way to ramble. This was more interesting the first time, when Ms. Treble told us."

Masha wasn't feeling the cute factor today. "The dogs are much more useful than the rabbits," she muttered as Bernadette droned on. She didn't miss the twitches of annoyance from Ms. Treble every time Bernadette said something that skated the line of being offensive.

"She isn't a fan of the dogs, that's for sure," Halli remarked, wrinkling her nose in distaste.

"I still don't think it's fair that Devi has to stay outside." Masha spoke quietly, not wanting to earn a rebuke from Bernadette. The crabby rabbit handler really had it in for the German Shepherd puppy.

Halli shrugged. "If it was up to me, I'd let her in. The rabbits are fine with us Wechselbalg, so I don't think a puppy is going to scare them."

Mischa picked up a wide-toothed comb to deal with a particularly matted clump. "How do they get so tangled?

Ugh." She teased the clump free and deposited it in her basket, lowering her voice to a whisper. "We could always sneak her in."

Yana frowned, also speaking quietly. "How would we do that? The handlers are always here."

Masha grinned. "Not at night, they're not."

"Fair enough," Yana conceded. "But how do we get down here without being noticed? Meredith would know, and we'd get caught. I'm not getting involved in an escapade. It was a big mistake not telling Ms. Dukes when you discovered the plot in Wales, so I would think you'd learned your lesson about sneaking around."

Masha and Mischa shared a glance, turning to Yana with their hands up in mock capitulation. "Okay, we won't sneak Devi in!"

Yana gave them her sternest look before returning her attention to her rabbit. "You'd better not."

"It would probably be easier to sneak one of the rabbits out anyway," Masha mused. "Then the rules haven't been broken and Devi gets her wish."

Yana rolled her eyes. "Whatever. Just don't involve *me*."

"Forget that," Halli broke in. "What are we going to do about Tina and Ron? The last week has been horrendous. And has anyone seen much of Maxim?"

"Maxim's got a lot to deal with at the moment," Yana told her. "He's meeting us at the library later. You are right about Tina and Ron, though. They keep arguing, and I feel torn between the two of them."

"It's affecting all of us," Masha agreed. "Although I don't see what the problem is."

"I think Tina has it right." Mischa flipped her hair. "She

shouldn't have to compromise her prospects just to save Ron's hurt feelings. If they're meant to be together they'll meet again when the time is right."

Halli shrugged. "I just wish they'd waited until after graduation to get all dramatic about it."

"Less chatting, more grooming, ladies," Bernadette called.

Masha raised her eyebrow just a fraction as they got back to work and Mischa winked at her.

It was on.

QBBS *Meredith Reynolds*, Etheric Academy, Library

Maxim sat waiting for the others to arrive for their study session. The students had all finished for the day and Yana had organized an evening meetup while the library was quiet. He'd gotten here early and ended up staring at the galaxy as it swirled softly outside the picture window. However, he wasn't really seeing any of it. His mind was elsewhere.

A movement in the lobby below caught his attention, snapping him from his brooding. Tina was gesticulating angrily at Ron as they crossed the floor toward the double staircase on their way up to the library.

He wondered what Ron had done to get himself in the doghouse this time. Those two had been arguing a lot since the Gate.

Maxim didn't want to dwell on the Gate. He pushed the thought aside quickly, before the pain that even thinking about it caused could blindside him. He had resolved to harden his heart, and that meant diverting himself every time thoughts of his father reared up.

The doors opened, giving Maxim the distraction he needed. Tina stormed in with a face like thunder, followed a minute later by Ron.

"What's up?" he asked, looking from one to the other.

Tina jabbed an accusing finger in Ron's direction. "Ask *him*!"

Ron glared back at her, his face flushed.

Maxim held up his hands. "Sorry, didn't mean to make it worse."

"It's not your fault, Maxim," Tina told him, putting her bag down at a workstation and switching it on.

"It's not *my* fault either!" Ron cried. "*You're* the one who's making it impossible. It can't get any worse!"

Much to Maxim's relief, Mischa came into the library at that moment.

Mischa assessed the awkward scene in one quick look. "What's going on? Are you two fighting again?"

"Ron thinks I should forget about studying."

"No, I don't!" Ron cried.

Mischa tilted her head. "What! Why?"

Tina sent icy daggers Ron's way. "So I can wait around for *him*."

Ron hit his forehead with his hand. "That's *not* what I said! I said that you're taking on too many classes and you won't have time for anything, not just me!"

Tina arched an eyebrow. "'When is our time?' *That's* what you said. 'Why don't you drop a few classes so I get to see you when I'm not doing my thing?'"

Maxim shook his head at Ron in disbelief. "You didn't really ask her to do that. Not cool, dude."

Ron went red. "It's not like that! I get one shot at impressing the R&D team. It's hard enough knowing they see me as a kid. If I flake now, it just proves it! My armor is going to save lives, but if I'm not on the team it's never going to get made."

Maxim grimaced. "It doesn't sound easy, but you can't ask Tina to put her life on hold just to make you happy."

"Yeah, Ron." Mischa snickered. "What fantasy are you living in? You sound like some 1950s mudball sitcom."

Tina huffed impatiently. "I understand that you need to prove yourself, Ron. I really do! What I *don't* understand is why you expect me to stay here and...and do *what*, exactly? I have my own life to build. Do you hear me asking you to stay at school with me? Not to disappear for days at a time while you're on a project?"

Ron shook his head reluctantly.

"No!" Tina emphasized her point by banging her hand on the desk. "Do you know why? Because I *respect* you enough to let you find your own way. Maybe you should try doing the same for me."

Ron's mouth opened and closed. He turned on his heel and stormed toward the door. "Screw this! Do what you want, Tina. You were going to anyway." He slammed the door behind him.

"Sheesh, I've seen tripwires less tightly-strung than him." Mischa looked at Tina's screen. "What are you studying, anyway?"

Tina laughed and waved a hand at the screen. "What, this? Nonlinear ordinary differential equations." She shrugged, seeing the blank look on her friend's face. "It's math for engineering."

Mischa screwed up her face as she attempted to work out what possible use the squiggles on the screen could be to an engineer. "Nope, it may as well be in Yollin. I'll stick to practicing how to win at conversation with strangers who have an agenda, thanks."

Tina turned back to her workstation. "It's not too bad. How's it going with the rabbit project? I'm almost regretting not taking the class now."

"Grooming the rabbits is more fun than poking strands of hair into tubes and testing them for hours on end."

Tina snickered. "Why did you take the class, then?"

Mischa shrugged. "I needed a science credit and it looked to take the least time and labor. The class has been boring, but the rabbits are kind of cute. And the plants and ecologies level is, well, flat-out *interesting*. It's like its own world, and the adults there are all so dramatic! Bernadette still won't let Devi in, so Masha and Yana stayed behind after everyone left to help her today. Masha said she would get information out of her."

"Information?" Maxim asked, suddenly interested. "What kind of information? Why?"

Mischa shrugged. "Beats me. They'll be here soon, so you can ask her."

They didn't have to wait long. The door swung open, and Masha and Yana entered the library. Their heads were together and they were deep in hushed conversation as they crossed the room.

Mischa called to her sister, "Hey, what's happening?"

Masha's eyes shone with anger. "That ridiculous woman!"

Yana nodded, surprising Maxim and Tina.

"It's not like you to see the worst in someone, Yana," Maxim responded. "What has this woman done to make you both so angry?"

Yana's face was troubled. "She's just so *petty*. We stayed behind to help and she didn't even thank us! And she says the most horrible things about Yelena."

Tina's eyes flashed as she looked up. "What does she have against Yelena?"

"I'm not exactly sure, but she had plenty to say about Yelena getting some kind of preferential treatment over her." Yana shrugged and took a seat at the workstation next to Tina's.

Masha scowled. "You didn't hear her when she thought we were out of earshot. Guess she forgot I'm a Wechselbalg. I heard her bitching to Jainey that she would never let Devi in, and she didn't care if the Queen was unhappy with her. Ugh."

Mischa examined her nails. "She's not important enough for the Queen to take notice of. If you ask me, she's just bitter because she has a thing for Bobcat."

Everyone cracked up at that.

"So she's taking it out on Devi?" Tina surmised once the laughter died down. "What a nasty and small-minded thing to do!"

"I know, right?" Masha agreed. "I think we should keep an eye on her. The dogs all use the space down there to exercise. And what's up with Ron? He stomped past us without so much as a hello."

Maxim looked away. He had no intention of adding to the drama between Tina and Ron.

Tina flushed and muttered darkly under her breath. She stood and grabbed her things. "I'm going back to the dorm. I'm all done here."

She left without another word, her head down.

Maxim pushed away from the window. "I'm going to go too. I have early training tomorrow."

"Wait up, Maxim," Yana called. "I'll see you tomorrow," she told Masha and Mischa as she ran off, leaving the twins alone in the library.

"Way to kill the mood, sis." Mischa snickered.

Masha threw up her hands. "What did I say? Never mind, we'd better get back to the dorm and get some sleep. I have a plan about how to get a rabbit..."

QBBS *Meredith Reynolds*, Etheric Academy, Delta Class Dormitory

Masha frowned at her twin in the darkness. "Shhh, you'll wake Ksenia!"

She grabbed the carryall she'd placed at the end of her bed earlier and silently picked her way across the dorm. She grabbed her sister's hand. "Stop wasting time. Come *on*!"

Mischa stifled a giggle with her free hand and let Masha pull her out of the sleeping area. "I just find this whole thing too funny," she whispered after she'd shut the door behind them.

Masha turned on her penlight, resting it on the table while she took two soft bundles of clothing out of her carryall. She shook one out and pulled on the dark form-fitting all-in-one jumpsuit, leaving the other items aside for the moment. "What's so funny about it?"

"We're sneaking out in the middle of the night to kidnap a bunny so our friend the talking puppy can meet it. Life doesn't get more absurd than that."

Masha pulled a hood over her hair and tied a scarf around her face. Last were the gloves. "We have to get there without getting caught first." She grinned at her sister, checking her clothing to make sure there were no gaps.

Mischa gaped at her twin. "You can't walk around looking like that!"

Masha snorted. Trust Mischa to come out with something like that. "I've got the same for you. Make sure you're covered. You don't want to get covered in grease stains."

Mischa paled, pulling on the clothing and tying her hair back hastily. "Grease stains?"

"Uh-huh." Masha was matter of fact. She waited for Mischa to finish before opening the door to the corridor a crack and peering through to make sure nobody was there. "How else do you expect to get away with roaming around the *Meredith Reynolds* in the middle of the night, or to make it in and out without Bernadette catching us? We have to be sneaky, so we're going through the maintenance tunnels."

"I thought we were going to take the tram," Mischa complained. "You didn't mention anything about getting dressed up like ninjas and creeping around in dirty tunnels when you said you had a plan."

"And get busted? No way. Stay here if you like, but I'm

on a mission for Justice." Masha opened the door a little wider and stepped into the corridor, then looked back at her sister. "Are you coming?"

Mischa sighed and reluctantly followed. "*Fiiine*, but I want a spa day when this is done."

"Whatever. We'll bring Devi if she wants to come with us."

Quiet returned to the Delta Class dormitory, but all was not as it appeared. A silent conversation was going on where nobody else could hear it.

Are you sure about this, ADAM? The appropriate course of action would be to inform the school administrators before the students leave the Academy grounds.

>>Normally I would agree, Meredith, but after you brought up Masha's conversation with Yana in the cafeteria I had to get Bethany Anne's take on the problem. She wants me to find out what this young woman is made of.<<

What she is 'made of?' I do not understand.

>>Her fortitude, Meredith. I believe she would serve faithfully and well as a Guardian, but she dreams of something more. I may have a solution, providing she's got the mettle for the job. Besides, the only reason Bernadette isn't letting Devi in to see the rabbits is because she and Yelena are feuding.<<

That is...illogical.

>>Which is exactly why I intervened before you contacted Diane and Dorene. Let the kids have a little fun. I'll keep my eyes on them.<<

Your eyes? Oh, good one, ADAM. That's funny.

>>*Glad you think so, Meredith. I'll be here all week.*<<

ADAM followed the twins on the security cameras. They crept down the staircase and through the shadows of the lobby, then into the administrative wing toward the service tunnels that would eventually take them to the ecologies level.

He often amused himself this way when Bethany Anne was sleeping or busy. Although he respected the privacy of the humans aboard the *Meredith Reynolds*, he had taken to observing their comings and goings in the public spaces in an attempt to better understand them and improve the accuracy of his heuristic algorithms.

He hadn't counted on the enjoyment factor. Humans were fascinatingly illogical. Even *he* had trouble predicting the outcomes of their behaviors sometimes.

Now and then TOM would join him, and the two of them would compare the social interactions of the humans to memorable scenes from TV shows they had both seen. This time he was solo, since he had a purpose in allowing the teenagers to get up to their shenanigans.

Masha Kosolov didn't know it, but she was being interviewed.

Masha wanted to walk the line, and if that was where she belonged then ADAM would do his level best to point her in the right direction. She had certainly proven herself to be brave and resourceful during the siege at the castle, but did she possess the other qualities required for the hard road ahead?

He sent a message to Bernadette.

He guessed he'd find out.

CHAPTER TEN

Q BBS *Meredith Reynolds*, **Residential Area**

Peter glanced down at his tablet to make sure he had the address right. "Meredith, would you let them know I'm here, please? And start recording. I may have to refer back to this interview later."

Recording now, Meredith replied through his implant.

He waited patiently until the door opened to reveal an aproned elderly woman whose wispy white hair was twisted up in a messy bun above her rosy face.

"Oh, what a handsome young man!" she cooed. "You must be Commander Silvers."

"That's me, ma'am," he replied, blushing a little. The older ladies always embarrassed him. "I hope it's not too late to bother you?"

"Nonsense, come inside. I'm about to put supper out, if you'd like to join me? And call me Greta."

"Thank you, and call me Peter." He followed her inside, all the way back into a steamy kitchen. The aroma was heavenly, reminding him he was overdue for a meal. "Is that borscht I smell?"

"You bet it is! Sit yourself down. It's ready." She ladled out a bowlful and placed it on the table in front of him, then served herself and put a basket of rolls out before sitting opposite him. "Now what can I do for you?"

Peter nodded as he tasted his soup, the rich flavors playing across his palate. "Oh, that's *good*. Yeah, I wanted to get an idea of where you found our mystery Wechselbalg to try to find his people so he isn't alone. What can you tell me about him?"

Greta frowned in thought. "Not much that I haven't already said." She offered him the basket of rolls before taking one herself, ripping a piece from the crust and dipping it in her soup. "He came from nowhere. I did not know such things as vampires and Wechselbalg existed outside my baba's stories until I carted him home and watched his wounds heal before my eyes."

Peter let a small smile slip out. "I bet you were surprised, hey?"

Greta slapped the table and threw her head back, cackling. "Surprised? Oh, that's a *good* one! You could say that. Visitors were not common where I came from, you know. It was strange enough to see an unexpected person at all, never mind one who howled at the moon."

Peter made a face. "So you wouldn't know of any Wechselbalg near where you lived?"

Greta shook her head. "Only rumors of *Arkhangelsk*–Archangel, to the west. When I was young we were told stories about that place when the nights drew in."

Peter nodded. "That's okay. What about the man himself? How long did you look after him by yourself?"

She made a see-saw gesture with her hand. "Around a year or so, maybe?"

"Uh-huh, and did he ever say anything that gave you a clue about where he came from?"

Greta chewed thoughtfully. "Not while he was with me. It was when we got here that he became too much for me to handle. Before then he used to sit quietly on my porch watching the seasons pass. When we came up here, *that* was when things got interesting."

"What do you mean, 'interesting?'" Peter asked.

Greta shook her head sadly. "He'd always been withdrawn, but on the day we arrived he reacted to something and that was it. I'd never seen him so upset!" Her eyes misted over as she recalled the day.

Peter leaned in a touch, wanting to know more. "What happened next?"

"He ran off. I called for help, and the station computer sent a nice young man called Tim to restrain him while we waited for the paramedics to arrive."

I am much more than just a computer, Meredith interjected.

I know that, Peter replied with a chuckle. *Give her a break, she's old. And pull the relevant records from that day and send them to my tablet, please.*

Already done.

Greta didn't notice Peter's momentary distraction, still lost in her recollection. "I go and visit most days, but as you can see, I'm no *devushka*. I worry what will become of him after I'm gone if he does not remember who he is." She sighed, dropping the remains of her roll into her bowl.

"Don't worry," he reassured her. "He's got me to look out for him now."

Greta's kind eyes crinkled as she broke into a smile and reached out with a liver-spotted hand to pinch his cheek. "You're a good boy. He is lucky to have you." She got up to take the bowls to the sink.

"Let me," Peter told her, getting up. "It's the least I can do after you shared your meal with me."

When he left a short while later Greta pressed a package of homemade honey cakes into his hands as he said goodbye, extracting a promise of a return visit before she hugged him and sent him on his way.

The visit hadn't given him much to go on. But he had a photo of the man on his tablet and he hoped now that he had an idea of where the man had come from he could zero in on the right community to begin his search.

QBBS *Meredith Reynolds*, Plants and Ecologies Level, Rabbit Habitat

Masha clung to the shadows in the passage between the rabbit and chicken habitats.

She smelled a familiar musky perfume.

"Get back! It's Bernadette," she whispered to Mischa She pushed her twin behind her as her sensitive ears picked up footsteps nearby.

They held their breath and pressed themselves against the wall as a silhouette crossed the mouth of the passage, only releasing it a few seconds later after Bernadette walked by without noticing anything amiss.

Mischa made a move but Masha held her back, her low voice muffled by the scarf around her face. "Not that way, Mish." She turned and set off toward the other end of the passage, pulling her sister along by her sleeve.

"Where are you going?" Mischa hissed. "The entrance is this way."

Masha shook her head. "We're not going in through the front. There's a camera."

Mischa stamped her foot. "Why are you so bothered about the cameras? We would have been in and out already if you weren't being so paranoid!"

"Because we don't want to leave any evidence that we did this. Now come on!" She set off at a jog without waiting to see if her twin followed, stopping when she reached the chain-link gate at the far end of the wall that surrounded the grassy area at the back of the building.

She sprang up, grabbed the top bar, and hauled herself over, landing in a crouch and catching her breath while she waited for Mischa to join her on the other side.

"Ugh, my nail broke. That's my manicure, ruined!" Mischa complained, landing beside her. She held the offending nail up in Masha's face. "Why do I let you drag me into these things?"

Masha shrugged. "We're going for a spa day, remember?"

"What about the rabbit? We can't leave it in the dorm. Ksenia would squeal on us in a heartbeat if she found it."

Masha set off toward the sunroom at the rear of the building. "We'll have returned it by then. We can hide it in a cupboard; make it comfortable. I'll sneak it back in when we come to groom them after lunch." She hurried along the fence line, keeping her body low to stay out of sight until she reached the door.

Mischa was right behind her. "So how are we getting in? You planning on sneaking in through a window or climbing up to the roof?"

"I thought we'd just go in through the door." Masha snickered. She shone her penlight on the keypad and pressed six numbers in quick succession, followed by the hash key.

The pad beeped and the door clicked.

Mischa's face was priceless "How...?"

"I watched Bernadette while we were bringing the rabbits in after the class left," Masha told her sister with a knowing wink. She pulled the door open. "We're in. Let's go hunt a wabbit..."

They tiptoed down the corridor toward the rabbit enclosure, hyper-aware of the slightest noise as they crept through the unlocked door into the place where the rabbits slept.

The enclosure had rows of hutches stacked three high. Earlier that week Bernadette had told the students that they adjoined to simulate a warren.

Masha took out her penlight and switched it on, indicating to Mischa to do the same. "Split up. We need to find where the rabbits are huddled. Let's find one and get out of here before we get caught."

They went in opposite directions and peered into the hutches.

"Over here," Masha called softly. She bent down and

reached inside the hutch to scoop up the nearest rabbit. Its fluff tickled her nose. She cradled it carefully before placing it in the kitty-carrier she had borrowed from Tina to keep the rabbit safe. "I've got one. Let's get out of here."

"Good, it's getting late," Mischa huffed. "Some of us get cranky without enough beauty sleep!"

As they turned to leave a noise from the corridor froze them in their tracks. It was followed by a roving flashlight beam hitting the glass panel in the door.

"Hide!" Masha grabbed her sister's shoulder, dragging her behind a row of hutches.

The flashlight got brighter as its owner got closer. Mischa squirmed under Masha's panicked grip. "Ow!"

"Shhh, they'll hear us!" Masha peeped around the hutch as the door handle moved.

Crap, I left the hutch open! She left Mischa and dashed back to the hutch to close it as the door began to open.

With no time to make it back across the room, she had no choice but to crouch behind the hutch and hope that whoever was coming in hadn't seen the movement.

The flashlight swung over the room, and Masha wrinkled her nose as the scent of musk hit her.

Bernadette grumbled as she left, "There's nobody here. Busybody computer telling me how to run my rabbitry. I just forgot to lock up again..."

She thought Bernadette was somewhat ungrateful, although if it meant she would leave without examining the room too hard then who was Masha to argue?

The relief she felt when Bernadette shut the door was shattered when she heard the unmistakable sound of a key turning in the lock. She cursed softly.

"Are we trapped?" Mischa whispered. "Masha, I don't want to get in trouble."

"Me either," Masha replied. "But I didn't bring the right tools to open the door." She surveyed the locked room, looking for a way to get out that didn't involve breaking down the door. "The window! We will have to escape through there."

Mischa looked at the high window doubtfully. "How are we going to get all the way up there?"

Masha grinned. Her sister wasn't going to like this one bit. "Time for a quick change. Do you think you can jump that high in your wolf form?"

Mischa shook her head, tears filling her eyes. "You know I can't," she wailed. "We're going to get caught and expelled from the Academy and then where will we be, huh? Mom and Dad will murder us both!"

Masha comforted her sister the best way she knew how —she thumped her in the arm.

"*Ow!* What was that for?"

"To stop you from losing it," Masha growled. "*I* can make the jump, so suck it up. We need to get back to the Academy before we're missed." She swiftly undressed, tying her clothing into a bundle that could be tossed through the window and went to stand under the opening with her hands laced together. "Come on, Mish. I'll give you a boost and pass the rabbit and my stuff up to you, then I'll change and jump."

Mischa made a face but did as she was told.

A few minutes later they crept back to the gate and repeated the process, this time with Masha in her human form. They hopped the gate one at a time before scurrying back through the shadows to the maintenance tunnels.

"We made it!" Mischa leaned against the wall, breathing hard.

Masha checked on the rabbit in her bag. "Not yet. When we're safely in our beds, *then* we've made it."

She set off down the tunnel at a wary jog with Mischa close behind.

QBBS *Meredith Reynolds*, Etheric Academy, Delta Class Dormitory

Morning came far too soon for Masha.

She forced herself out of bed, rubbing the sleep from her eyes as she walked into the communal area to check on the rabbit before Ksenia woke up and found it first.

Mischa was already there. "Masha, did you move the rabbit?"

"No," Masha replied, confused. "It isn't where we left it?" She noted that the room was messier than usual. All of the cushions were scattered and the sofa had been pulled away from the wall.

"The cupboard door was open and it's gone."

They searched high and low, under and around the furniture and in every nook and cranny of the dorm. The rabbit was nowhere to be seen.

Masha spotted a scrap of fluff sticking to the arch between the carved feet of the bookcase. She tugged the fluff out and sniffed it. "Yep, that's our bunny." She bent down to look, seeing something shiny at the back but no sign of the rabbit.

She pulled the bookcase out, letting out a low moan when she saw what was behind it. "Mish, you better come and see."

The bookcase hid an air duct around two feet square. The vent cover was missing, and there was a small pile of rabbit droppings at the mouth of the duct, and a larger pile of discarded candy wrappers on the floor beneath.

She poked the empty candy wrappers on the floor with her toe, revealing the missing vent cover beneath them.

"What are we going to do?" Mischa lamented. "We can't go in there!"

Ksenia came out from the sleeping area, stretching and yawning. She took in the mess, the hastily-shoved-aside furniture, and the twins trying to appear nonchalant, and treated them to an icy look. "What's all this noise? Some of us are trying to sleep, you know. And why are you both staring at the wall?

Masha reddened. "It's nothing. But if you see a rabbit in the dorm, don't panic."

Ksenia frowned. "What have you two gotten yourselves into this time? I swear, since you started hanging out with the Alpha Class you've both changed. Now you've brought a rodent into the school and let it escape?"

Mischa scowled at Ksenia. "At least we're *doing* something! You just follow Tina's mom around with your puppy eyes, hoping she'll adopt you or something."

Masha sucked in a breath. "Too far, sis," she told Mischa. It wasn't unlike her twin to turn bitch when she was scared or anxious. However, Ksenia really did have Cheryl Lynn's ear and Masha wouldn't put it past her classmate to drop news of them into it to gain favor. "I'm sorry for what Mischa said. She didn't mean it."

Ksenia's eyes narrowed. "Yes, well, let's see what the administrators think about you stealing a rabbit and letting it loose in the Academy, shall we?"

Masha wished her sister had kept her mouth shut. "Ksenia, you wouldn't! We did it for Devi. We'll find the rabbit, I swear."

"Watch me," Ksenia threatened. "But seeing as you were doing it for Devi, I'll give you a break this time. Find that rabbit and take it back by the end of today or else I'm going to Dorene and telling her everything." She turned on her heel and stomped off, stopping at the door to look back at them. "Have fun crawling around in the vents, *Mischa*." With one final vicious look she slammed the door behind her.

Masha sighed and looked at Mischa. "Well, that tears it. You're going to need your ninja suit again, Misch."

Mischa scowled. "We're not going to the salon today, are we?"

QBBS *Meredith Reynolds*, Medical Level, Psychiatric Wing

Maxim left Doctor Dietrich's office feeling worse than before he'd arrived. Today the 'f' word had come up, and Maxim had been low enough that he'd told the doc everything—how he felt about his father, his future, and all the things that had happened to him in the last year. It had all come pouring out like bile, and now he had everything churning at the front of his mind.

How was this supposed to help?

He regretted talking to the doctor today. Opening up had laid him bare, broken down the walls he'd built to barricade his broken heart. It had left him defenseless. His heart pounded against his ribs, completely at odds with his calm exterior.

He bent at the waist, bracing his hands on his knees as the pangs of emotion tore at him. His head throbbed and his stomach churned with the onslaught.

He needed to get out of there. His footfalls echoed along the corridor as he ran, ignoring the elevator in favor of the stairs so he didn't have to wait.

He didn't know where he was headed. All he knew was that he didn't want to go to his uncle's quarters or to the Academy dorm.

He wanted to go *home*.

It was too much. Maxim was in no shape to regain control. His eyes turned yellow unnoticed as he reached the bottom of the stairs and threw open the stairwell door.

He caught sight of his hand as he let go of the handle. It didn't look quite right, but the thought was lost as he crashed into the long corridor leading from the psych wing to the lobby. He scanned the corridor, wondering briefly where all the people were running to.

Maybe they were hurting inside, just like him. Maybe they needed to run, too.

He roared his anguish, picking up speed as he exited the corridor into the lobby. The people here were running too. What was making everyone scream?

The scent of fear in the air snapped him out of his blind run and he skidded to a halt, looking around in confusion as his Guardian instincts kicked in. He forgot his pain in the face of a threat to the innocent.

He turned in a circle to look for the threat, but he saw nothing.

"What's wrooooong with everyooone?" His voice sounded unfamiliar to his ears, but he had no time to consider why. A monster shot across the lobby toward him, moving so fast Maxim couldn't make out what it was. It was bigger than him; he was sure of that much. Was this the threat?

Then nothing mattered.

"Leave these people alooone!" Maxim roared. "They are miiine to prooooteeect!"

He sprang at the monster, determined to safeguard the terrified people. He ducked the oncoming beast's swipe, delivering a double-punch to its stomach that would have killed a human.

"Maaaxim," it demanded, skipping back and cuffing his head. "Stand doooown."

Was this a trap? How did the monster know his name?

He shook his head in confusion and launched himself at the trickster. The intruder easily deflected Maxim's teeth and claws and Maxim snarled, his rage at his opponent fueling his determination as he attacked again.

Again he was repelled. A voice called from the side, distracting him.

"It's no good, Commander, he won't quit. He's too damn stubborn. You'll have to knock him out."

Something smashed into the side of Maxim's face and the last thing he saw was the floor rushing up to meet him.

His next recollection was waking up on the lobby floor with Craig and Commander Silvers standing over him.

He blinked to clear his vision. The unexpected angle of the room jarred him. "What happened?"

Craig held a hand out. "You okay, buddy? You took a pretty good punch to the jaw there."

"Was that what it was?" Maxim accepted Craig's offered hand and pulled himself up. He rubbed the side of his face, feeling the tenderness where he'd taken the hit. It wasn't broken, or if it had been it was already healing. His head swam.

Peter guided him to a nearby bench. "Sit down for a minute. How do you feel?"

Maxim assessed himself gingerly. "I'm uninjured, but hungry and tired. Did I shift?"

Craig let out a low whistle. "*Did* you!"

Peter shushed him. "What do you remember, Maxim?"

"The people; they were screaming."

"They do that when there's an angry Pricolici running around," Peter told him solemnly.

Maxim nodded, remembering the monster before it laid him out. "I fought it, I remember that much."

Craig gaped. "Dude, *you* were the Pricolici! The one you fought was Commander Silvers."

"What?" Maxim was dumbfounded. "I don't under-stand." He remembered how the Pricolici had known his name and how everything had seemed different as he fought. "Oh. *Oh*… I had no idea that was even..."

"I know you're going through some heavy stuff right now." Peter patted his shoulder in sympathy. "You must have been feeling something pretty extreme to trigger the dormant programming in your nanocytes." He looked Maxim over. "The question is how? You went into the Pod-doc when you first got here, right?"

Maxim nodded, his eyelids drooping as exhaustion took over.

"Okay, we're gonna have to get you back into a Pod-doc to get checked out." He looked at Craig. "I have to go and deal with the situation that brought us here in the first place. You take Maxim up to the med bay while I handle it." He patted Maxim on the shoulder again. "When I get back we'll get to the bottom of this, Maxim. Okay?"

Maxim nodded, which was all he was capable of at that point. He thought he remembered seeing his fingernails replaced with impossibly sharp claws. He looked blankly at his hands in his lap, his head growing heavy.

He lay down across the bench, half-listening to Commander Silvers instruct Craig to keep Maxim within sight. The last thing he saw before sleep stole him away was Peter pointing at the vending machines across the lobby as he left. "And get some food for when he wakes up."

Peter hurried to Ward G, hoping that Maxim's diversion hadn't kept him from getting there before the mystery patient was sedated again.

He wanted to try to speak to him to see if he could glean any more clues about the man's origins before he went on the hunt for the man's past.

Nobody should have to live in torment like that.

By the time he got there the situation had been

contained. He saw Dwayne, the Guardian on duty, standing by the reception desk and went over to get a report. He nodded at Lucy, who was on duty, before turning to Dwayne. "I got your message. Is he awake?"

The Guardian shook his head. "He's out cold, sir. We had to sedate him."

"*Gott Verdammt*! Won't drugging him over and over like this make him worse?"

Lucy came out from behind the desk as she answered him. "No, the sedation between active periods actually gives his brain a rest and speeds healing time."

Peter frowned. "So why aren't you keeping him sedated until he's fully healed?"

"It doesn't work like that." Lucy chuckled as she passed him a tablet. "Here, see his notes? The brain is a complicated organ. Wakeful periods are just as important to the healing process as resting ones. Besides, he wasn't under any sedation at all today because we needed him alert for the scans. I was bringing him back when he reacted to something. I was lucky Guardian Dwayne was here to restrain him while I administered the tranquilizers."

Peter looked up from the tablet. That was the second time he'd heard that phrase. Only a small part of what he was reading made sense to him anyway, and Lucy may have inadvertently given him a clue. "He reacted to something?"

She nodded. "Yeah. He'd been calm all morning, but all of a sudden he leapt out of the wheelchair and shouted, "Why?'"

Peter grinned and handed the tablet back. "Finally, something I can work with."

He left the ward, taking his tablet out and pulling up the video from the other times Ilya had escaped. He replayed each incident as he walked, beginning with the first time it had happened.

The man sat in a chair in the dayroom of the long-term ward, staring at the unfinished jigsaw puzzle on the table before him with the glazed eyes of the heavily medicated. Peter zoomed in, watching closely for the moment when he went from catatonic to Defcon One.

Peter saw it. A twitch of the man's nose, and a fraction of a second later the detached expression was replaced by one of utter and desperate longing.

He bolted upright, knocking the chairs and tables over as he made a break for the door. Peter froze the video and checked the other incidents.

They were all pretty much the same as the first. The man was mostly calm and malleable, going about his daily routine as peacefully as the other patients on the ward. But no matter how calm he was, when he caught the scent he had to be restrained and sedated by the nurses.

"Meredith, take a look at these vids. What was happening around Medical at the same times the patient has tried to escape?"

Meredith answered through his implant almost instantly. *There were twenty-three thousand six hundred and seventy-two separate events across the level for the first time stamp alone, Peter. If you tell me what you are looking for perhaps I can narrow it down.*

"Look at the moment before he goes bananas," he told Meredith. "He's reacting to a scent. He thinks the person he's looking for is here, so let's try and find out if he's right."

We can certainly try, although a scent is not much to go on since I cannot process olfactory data. Meredith paused. *I think the more pressing concern is how young Maxim managed to unlock his Pricolici. A hundred thousand Pricolicis rampaging across the station would be disastrous for us all.*

Peter stopped walking. How *had* Maxim gained his third form?

With a few exceptions, all of the Wechselbalg had been in the Pod-doc for reprogramming by TOM to prevent the Pricolici pathways from being activated. It was safer for everyone that way. If there was any chance the programming could fail they needed to get on that.

Like yesterday.

"You're right, Meredith." The mystery man would have to wait for now. He hurried to the elevator, which Meredith had the doors open for him.

"Contact Bethany Anne. If TOM's programming has failed, we need to know why."

CHAPTER ELEVEN

Q BBS *Meredith Reynolds*, **Etheric Academy, Alpha Class Dormitory**

Tina woke up and immediately noticed that Fudge wasn't on her bed.

The kitten wasn't on her own bed, either. She saw that the door to the sleeping area was ajar and groaned, standing up. She did a quick sweep of the room, but she couldn't see Fudge anywhere. "Where is she? Fudge?"

Ron was on the sofa when she entered the living area, engrossed in a thick manual. She ignored him and started looking under the furniture.

Ron put his manual down and got up. "What are you doing?"

"I'm looking for Fudge. Have you seen her?"

"Not since last night," Ron replied with a worried look. "Try shaking the kibble box. That usually brings her running."

Tina did as Ron suggested, but Fudge didn't appear. "Where *is* she?" Her frustration was rapidly turning to worry when there was a knock at the door. She opened it and Devi sauntered in followed by Kris, who was holding a squirming Fudge in her hands and getting clawed by the protesting kitten for her trouble.

"Ow!" She thrust Fudge at Tina. "Here you go. Someone left your door open and she got out."

Devi chuffed. "I found her destroying school property. I told you she was bad news!"

Tina took Fudge and cradled her close. "Thanks, Kris." Fudge began to purr, snuggling close to Tina.

"No worries," Kris told her. "I better go. See you later."

Devi sniffed moodily at Fudge. Then her puppy nose twitched and she yipped at Tina. "Can you smell that?"

"Human, Devi." Tina deadpanned, waving her finger in a circle around her nose.

Devi let out a barking laugh. "Oh, yes, I forget. Your nose doesn't work like mine. There is an interesting scent that requires my investigation. Would you care to join me?"

Tina snickered at the puppy, who was already moving away, drawn by whatever irresistible scent she was picking up. "You're funny, Devi. I have to get to class soon, and Fudge and I haven't had breakfast yet."

"Your loss," Devi replied, already halfway down the corridor. "Whatever the smell belongs to, my nose is telling me it'll be well worth finding!"

"Just stay out of trouble," Tina called as she shut the door.

She went over to Ron, holding Fudge up to chastise her. "You can't go wandering around like that!" Fudge mewed in return, which melted Tina's resolve. "Oh, I can't be mad at you. You're too cute!"

Ron laughed. "You spoil her."

"So I should," Tina retorted. "She's adorable."

Ron went to say something but stopped himself.

"Spit it out," Tina told him as she shook kibble into Fudge's bowl. The kitten began to crunch away happily.

Ron shrugged. "I don't think I should. You get mad every time I bring up the future."

Not this, again. Tina sighed mentally. It had gone on too long. They were going their separate ways and there was nothing that could be done about it.

"See, I only have to mention the word and you're rolling your eyes!"

Whoops. Tina sat down next to him on the sofa. "Ron, look... We're just making this painful. For both of us."

Ron opened his mouth to speak. "Tina..."

She waved his protest off. "No, Ron. I can't keep going around in circles. It's driving me crazy! What do you want, for us to run off together into the sunset? Be practical! Use the brain that attracted me to you in the first place and actually *think* about what you're asking me to do."

"I'm asking you to stay with me. To share my life," Ron declared.

Tina crossed her arms. "That's the problem. You want me to share *your* life. What about *my* life? Where does that fit in?"

"After we get married you can..." Ron faltered as her eyes pierced him.

"*Married?*" Tina was momentarily speechless. His suggestion that she delay her studies the other night had been bad enough, but *marriage*? Was that where he saw them going? "Is that what you were going to talk about, kids of our own?" She shook her head in disbelief. "Do you even *know* me? Next you'll tell me you want a steady job in finance. It would be less ridiculous than what just came out of your mouth."

Ron threw his hands up in despair. "What's wrong with knowing what you want from life?"

"We are seventeen, Ron! *Seventeen*! We have our whole lives ahead of us and you want us to decide on everything now? People change and grow, Ron. It's already happening." She sighed sadly. "We're through, and I think one of us should transfer to another dorm if you can't accept that."

Ron's head jerked in surprise. "Are you kidding?"

Tina shook her head. "No, Ron, I'm serious. I can't do this anymore and it doesn't matter how many times we have this conversation—we aren't getting anywhere. I'm not going to avoid the inevitable. Please just accept it too, so we can get past all of this and be friends again." Fudge jumped onto her lap and Tina wrapped her arms around her, letting the kitten nuzzle her. She refused to meet Ron's searching gaze. "If you can't be my friend right now, then just leave me alone until you can."

Ron's face grew redder, but a few frustrated huffs were all he could manage. He got up without another word and walked stiffly out of the dorm, slamming the door behind him.

Tina sobbed into Fudge's soft fur while the kitten licked her tears away with her sandpaper tongue. Fudge mewed, not understanding what was wrong with her human. Tina let out a choked laugh and tickled the kitten's chin. "I know, Fudge," she told the kitten in a small voice as she wiped her tears away. "I won't be sad forever. It sure hurts now, though…"

QBBS *Meredith Reynolds*, Medical Level

Craig sat by the Pod-doc that Maxim had been inside for the last few hours, waiting for Commander Silvers to get there. He sighed, thinking that he spent more time in this place than anywhere else.

Maybe he should have considered a career in orthopedics instead of the military. He stood to stretch his legs and leaned over to peer through the window at Maxim.

The doctor had explained to Craig earlier that there had been an unexpected fault in Maxim's nanocyte programming that had forced him into Pricolici mode. Maxim's first session in the Pod-doc had blocked the normal triggers—anger or protective instinct—but the hidden pathway, the one that had been triggered by the neurochemical overload caused by Maxim's grief, had remained viable.

All the Wechselbalg aboard were being checked for the same fault. If nothing else, Maxim's predicament had uncovered a potential ticking time bomb. What if that pathway was triggered at the wrong moment?

"Sneaky Kurtherian… Y'know what, there isn't a curse strong enough. I hope they only found it in you, dude," he murmured. "It'd be like a space-werewolf horror movie if every angry Wechselbalg aboard the *Meredith Reynolds* suddenly went Pricolici on our asses."

He heard a noise behind him and turned to see Commander Silvers and a nurse coming in through the door. "Hey, sir. What's the news?"

Peter nodded. "Nice situational awareness there, Craig. It's almost time for Maxim to come out of the Pod-doc, and I have another assignment for you."

"Sir?"

"First of all, get your ass down to the APA and start getting yourself back in shape for duty." Peter held a tablet out to Craig. "In the meantime, I have a little assignment for you—and maybe Maxim too if he's feeling up to it after he gets out of here. There's a man on the long-term psych ward; nobody knows who he is. I want you to show his picture to all the Russian Wechselbalg and see if you can find anyone who knows him, or *of* him."

Craig glanced quickly at the photo. "Of course, sir. Any other instructions?"

Peter thought about it for a moment. "Yeah. If you *do* find anyone who knows him, don't tell them he's here. Just report straight back to me. A lot of people lost or left family behind during the evacuation and I don't want to get anyone's hopes up."

"Sir." Craig nodded and made to leave the room. He looked back as he reached the door. "Sir, Maxim's gonna be okay, isn't he? He's kind of grown on me."

Peter placed a hand on the lid of the Pod-doc. "I hope so, Craig. Kid's gone through enough."

Craig looked at the photo of the man as he left. He looked kind of familiar, but he couldn't put his finger on why he thought so.

He left Medical wondering where the hell to start.

. . .

QBBS *Meredith Reynolds*, Etheric Academy, Ventilation System

Masha halted her slow crawl forward to flick away the rabbit droppings in her path.

"Ow, watch it!"

Masha twisted to look back at her sister. "Quit bumping into me! And stop talking so loudly; the echoes will get back to someone. We can't be far now. I can see where it opens up ahead."

She began shuffling along the narrow duct again, pausing now and then to flick the 'breadcrumbs' away as she progressed toward the junction.

Mischa huffed. "Yana was right, we shouldn't have done this. *Ow!*"

They reached the junction and Masha squirmed out of the duct, making use of the open space of the junction to stretch out her cramped muscles as Mischa struggled out of the duct to land a little less than gracefully. The poop trail had disappeared for now. "Where has the little stinker gone?"

Mischa shrugged.

"For crying out loud, Mish, use your *nose!*" Masha made a face and crouched to sniff at the mouth of each duct until she picked up the scent of the rabbit. "Oh..."

"What is it now? Mischa demanded.

"I can smell the rabbit, but I can smell Devi as well!"

She dove headfirst into the duct, calling behind her as she went, "Come on! We need to find them, and quickly!"

They shinnied through the duct and Masha was

rewarded with confirmation the rabbit had passed that way a few moments later when she came across a pile of droppings. She poked the pellets with her finger.

Still warm.

"Mish, we've nearly found it. These droppings are fresh."

"I know, I can smell it," Mischa retorted, giving Masha a little push to get her moving. "Come on, let's just get out of this stupid duct!"

They came to another junction, this one opening out onto rows of hissing pipes and ductwork. Steam from the pipes hung ominously in thick layers, diffusing the overhead lights.

Masha looked at the eerie halos along the ceiling. "We're down in the basement," she told her sister, who was staring at it all with a puzzled expression. "It's where all the utilities for the Academy come in." She cast her gaze around the floor, looking for any sign of the rabbit—or Devi, whose scent was stronger now that they were out of the duct. "We'll split up. You go left, I'll go right and we'll meet in the center."

Mischa looked uncertain.

"Come on, before Devi finds it and spoils her surprise!"

They split, Masha keeping low to peer under the rows of hissing pipes whilst keeping an eye out for Devi as she went up and down the rows. She crossed paths with Mischa when she got to the center.

They paused in the open space between the rows, Masha wiping the sweat from her forehead. "It's too hot in here. No rabbit?"

Mischa shook her head. "Not a sign, but I can *smell* it! Where has it gone?"

Masha closed her eyes and focused, searching out the rabbit scent amongst the many-layered basement smell.

"What are you doing?"

Masha opened her eyes and glared at her sister. "I was *trying* to concentrate."

Mischa put a hand on her chest in mock-horror. "Well, excuse me."

Masha rolled her eyes. "Whatever. Come on, I think it's somewhere this way." She moved off in the direction she'd indicated, scanning the floor as she went.

They were rewarded a few minutes later when Mischa spotted a tuft of white fur on a jutting pipe near the floor.

Mischa held it up, triumphantly accepting Masha's high-five. "We almost have it now!" They hurried on, keeping their eyes peeled for the next clue.

As the path split, Masha caught a twitch of movement out of the corner of her eye. "There," she whispered. "Look." She pointed to the end of the row, where the rabbit, whose nose was twitching, was perched on top of a mess of cables next to an open door.

Masha froze, not wanting to spook the rabbit into making a break for the dark corridor beyond the door. "Don't make any sudden moves, Misch."

"What do you think I am? Of course not! Now go and get that rabbit so we can get the hell out of here!"

Masha crouched as she advanced slowly toward the rabbit.

She was just about to cup her hands around it when a

shaggy black blur came bounding around the corner, yipping excitedly.

The rabbit bolted before Masha could grab it, moving faster than either of them had anticipated as the German Shepherd puppy gave chase with a happy howl.

"For Gloooory!"

She shot past them down the dark corridor in hot pursuit of the bouncing ball of fluff.

The twins yelled in unison. *"Devi! No!"*

The puppy skidded to a halt, her claws almost scritching grooves into the stone floor as she scrabbled for purchase...but it was too late. The rabbit was gone, fled through the open door into the maze of rooms beyond.

"Now we'll never catch it!" Mischa wailed.

"I'm sorry." Devi panted. "I didn't *mean* to chase it. It just sort of happened..."

CHAPTER TWELVE

Q BBS *Meredith Reynolds*, Etheric Academy, Lobby, Two Weeks Later

School was done for the day and Tina gripped Fudge's kitty carrier tightly as she descended the stairs on her way to see Marcus. She had a tricky assignment she needed his help with, so she and Fudge were going over to the BMW offices.

Fudge protested the lack of room in the carrier. The kitten had grown fast this last couple of weeks; Tina would have to stop by the pet store and pick up a bigger one if she was going to be taking care of Fudge for much longer.

She stopped to talk to Ms. Treble, who came out of the administrative wing just as Tina reached the bottom of the stairs.

"You on your way out, Tina?" the teacher asked.

"Uh-huh." She hoisted the carrier. "We'll be back by curfew, promise."

Ms. Treble smiled, peering into the carrier. Fudge

bumped her face against Ms. Treble's outstretched finger. "Oh, she's a darling."

Tina didn't miss the look of adoration in the teacher's eyes. "You like cats, Ms. Treble? Fudge is still looking for a forever home if you're interested." She offered the last a little reluctantly, realizing that if Ms. Treble said yes then she'd have to say goodbye to Fudge—and she didn't know if she wanted to do that just yet. "I mean, you don't have to or anything; it was just an idea."

The teacher looked at her thoughtfully for a moment. "I haven't time to housetrain a kitten and I'm still getting settled into my apartment, but if you'd like to hang on to her until she's independent I would love to give her a home. How does that sound?"

Tina grinned. "I'll have to run it by Marcus, but that sounds great, Ms. Treble."

She waved goodbye as she hurried off.

Katie watched Tina go before continuing on her way.

First love was never easy, and the discussion in the staffroom had turned to Tina's breakup with Ronnie Diamantz more than once over the last couple of weeks. Ronnie had moved to the Bravo dormitory, exchanging bunks with Halli Matteson.

Katie hadn't been the only one who had breathed a sigh of relief when the relationship had concluded without needing the faculty to intervene.

She snapped out of her daydream and swiped her key card over the lock on her front door. Maybe a cat was just what she needed. It would beat coming home to an empty apartment every night.

Tina needed the company more than she did right now, though. She could wait.

She sighed as she stepped over the half-unpacked boxes lining her hallway. She really needed to get to them if she would be bringing a cat home.

In the meantime, Katie had a mystery to solve—namely, to find out what the Kosolov twins were hiding. You didn't spend as long teaching as she had and miss the signs that a student was up to something.

And those two were *definitely* up to *something*.

QBBS *Meredith Reynolds*, Alpha Class Dormitory

Craig walked into the dorm to find Maxim with one foot braced against a chair, tying his bootlaces.

"You ready, dude?"

Maxim nodded. "Nearly."

When he'd finished, they left the dorm. Craig gave Maxim the once-over. "You sure you're up for this?"

Maxim gave him a look. "What, walking?"

Craig shoved Maxim lightly. "Nice to see they put a sense of humor in you while you were in the Pod-doc. That come for free, or did they charge you extra for it?"

Maxim returned Craig's shove. "It was free, dumbass. I told the docs how much time I have to spend with you, so they took pity on me and installed it while I was out. They said it was the least they could do to ease my suffering."

Craig's smile melted away. "Seriously, dude?"

Maxim nodded at his friend with a completely straight face. "Seriously."

Craig grinned. "You're an ass, Maxim. You had me scared for a minute."

"I've had time to recover." Maxim shoved his friend again. "Too scared to notice that Mischa keeps looking at you with gooey eyes?"

Craig laughed nervously, clapping Maxim on the back. "No idea what you're talking about. So, you ready for a wild goose chase, dude? I'm glad you're coming with, since I have no clue where to start. I think the commander only gave me this assignment to keep me occupied."

Maxim snickered. "You cannot blame him. Anything that keeps you out of Medical has to be a good thing, right?" He ducked Craig's playful swipe. "Anyway, I know a good place to start. Are you hungry?"

Craig raised an eyebrow. "Is a duck's ass watertight? Lead on."

Maxim steered them in the direction that would take them to the open court. "So, what is this wild goose chase?"

Craig shrugged. "There's a guy on the psych wing. The commander wants me to try to find his family, or at least someone who might know him. I'm gonna show his photo around, see what I turn up." He stopped and inhaled the aroma emanating from the store ahead of them. "Oh, man, it smells good in there."

Maxim nodded. "Best bakery on the rock. I haven't been here for a long time."

Craig heard a high bell tinkle as he pushed the door open. "The rock?"

"You know—we came from the mudball, now we live on the rock." He shrugged. "It could become a thing."

Craig shook his head slowly. "Meh, not feeling it." He opened the tablet and pulled up the image of the man as he approached the man behind the counter.

The man looked up from the book he was reading. "Guardians, welcome to my establishment. How can I help you?" He put his book down and his apron on.

"Is that *muraveynik?*" Maxim asked, practically drooling as he pointed to a hill-shaped cake near the back of the display cabinet.

"Made it myself this morning," the owner replied with a wide smile. "You look like a young man who hasn't had the taste of home in a while. Let me remedy that. What would you like?" Maxim pointed out various pastries, and the owner filled a box with his selections and passed it over the counter.

Maxim took the box with thanks and went to sit at one of the outdoor tables, leaving Craig to ask his questions and pay for breakfast.

"Do you know this man?" Craig showed the bakery owner the image on his tablet. "I'm trying to find anyone who knows him, his family if I can. "

The owner studied the photo on the screen for a long moment. "I can't say that I do. He doesn't look familiar. I'm sorry."

"No worries, thank you anyway." He took the tablet back and turned to leave. "Do you mind if I ask your customers?"

"Sure, go ahead," the owner replied.

Craig had no more luck with the rest of the bakery's

clientele. He made his way over to where Maxim sat demolishing the pastries he'd bought and dropped the tablet on the table. He peered into the box. "Hey, did you save me any?"

Maxim laughed. "You know what they say—" His mood switched as his eyes alighted on the tablet screen. "What is this?" He picked up the tablet and brought it to his face for a closer look.

Craig was instantly concerned. "It's the guy whose family I'm trying to track down for Commander Silvers. Why, what's up? You okay, dude?"

Maxim looked up, the color draining from his face. "This man—he looks just like my father."

Craig's mouth dropped open. "Are you sure?"

Maxim looked again, hardly believing what he was seeing. "I...yes. I think it is him? He looks different; older. You said he is in Medical? In the psychiatric wing? Why?"

Craig shook his head. "I don't know. The commander didn't give me much info." He took the tablet, holding it up to Maxim's face to compare the two. "You know, I thought he looked familiar somehow. Yeah, I can see it, maybe. Same stubborn-ass expression."

Maxim stood, pastries abandoned. "What are you waiting for? We need to go and tell him right now!" He dashed off, leaving Craig behind.

Craig grabbed the pastry box and ran to catch up. Maxim had made it halfway across the court before Craig fell into step beside him. "Dude, keep a lid on it."

The people around them glanced at Maxim with something approaching worry.

Maxim turned to him with an unfocused look. Craig

grabbed him and gave him a shake. "Listen, if you go Pricolici here the *only* place you'll be going is back in the Pod-doc. Get a grip!"

Maxim took a deep breath and slowed to a brisk walk. "Sorry, I just want to know if that man is my father. I'm not going to shift. You can check my eyes if you don't believe me."

Craig leaned in, seeing that Maxim's eyes were their usual medium-blue. "Fair enough. You don't know where the commander is, though."

Maxim made a face. "Oh, yeah. I wasn't thinking of that."

CHAPTER THIRTEEN

Q BBS *Meredith Reynolds*, Plants and Ecologies Level, Rabbit Habitat

Yana was over by the cornfield playing tag with Devi, Snow, and the Yollin, whom Meredith had told them was Captain Kael-ven T'chmon. Bernadette had yet to show up and let them in for the day's grooming and the class was getting bored.

Mischa and Masha were so busy whispering among themselves that they were unbothered by the wait.

"She's never usually late," Ms. Treble muttered. She took out her tablet. "Meredith?"

Meredith's voice came over the tablet speaker. "Good morning, Katie. How can I be of assistance?"

Ms. Treble frowned. "Bernadette isn't here to let us in. Can you tell me where she is, please?"

"Bernadette is currently inside the rabbit habitat, Katie," Meredith replied a moment later. "I have notified her of your arrival."

"Thank you, Meredith." Ms. Treble put her tablet away

and turned to the class. "I need to have a word with Bernadette before we go in. You can all take ten minutes and stretch your legs."

The door opened, revealing a scowling Bernadette. "What are you doing here?"

"We're due to begin taking samples this morning. Did you forget?"

Bernadette sneered. "I did not. Clearly, you missed my memo. Your students' assistance is no longer required."

Ms. Treble opened her mouth to speak. She glanced at the students and thought better of it. Instead, she marched over to the door and pushed Bernadette aside to enter before the rabbit handler had a chance to slam it in her face. "Your office, *now*," the teacher demanded in a tone that brooked no protest.

The twins snickered as Bernadette followed their teacher.

Yana and Halli headed for the cornfield, along with most of the rest of the class. Yana gestured to the twins. "Are you coming?"

The twins waved her off and watched them go, remaining on the low wall across from the habitat entrance where they'd sat when they got there.

Mischa kept her voice low. "What do you think Ms. Treble is saying to Bernadette?"

Masha's eyes twinkled. "I don't know. You wanna listen in?"

"Masha Kosolov, you are a bad influence."

Masha grinned. "You know I am. Anyway, you can't complain, dear sister. You'd have no fun at all without me."

Her eyes darted toward the wall, where Bernadette's office was. "Come on, the window is open."

They crept over to the side of Bernadette's office and stood on their tiptoes to get closer to the high window to hear what Ms. Treble was saying through the inch-wide gap it was open.

The teacher's voice was muffled. "So why aren't you letting my students in? Don't tell me you haven't appreciated the extra help these last few weeks."

"It's nothing to do with your students. Look at this."

They heard Ms. Treble gasp.

Masha silently cursed the wall for being between her and whatever Bernadette had just shown Ms. Treble.

"That's not...well. It's not good, that's for sure. What's the word from the labs?"

Bernadette sniffed. "That the gene is behaving in ways they hadn't anticipated. It's only an issue if they're left to breed unchecked."

They heard Ms. Treble sigh. "I see."

"I hope you also understand that if one of the expectant does gets out it would be disastrous for us all. I have no choice except to put the rabbitry on lockdown. Nobody in or out except myself and my staff."

The twins dropped down from the window and sat close together with their backs against the wall.

Masha was first to speak, her voice a whisper. "We *need* to find that rabbit."

"It isn't like we haven't been trying," Mischa hissed. "The basement is too big; we'll never find it!" She paused, considering what they'd just overheard. "What do you think Bernadette meant when she said the gene is behaving unexpectedly?"

Masha's face was solemn. "I don't know, but she mentioned breeding, so it can't be good."

Mischa twisted her hands together. "What if it's something really bad? What are we going to do, Masha?"

"We should tell the others. Ask them to help."

QBBS *Meredith Reynolds*, Guardians' APA

Peter saw Craig and Maxim enter the APA and racked his weights. He pointed to a clear space and grabbed a towel to wipe the sweat from his face and neck, dropping his towel in one of the baskets placed around for that purpose as he walked over to meet them.

"Hey, what's up? I thought you two'd be out showing that photo around today?"

"It's my father, sir," Maxim blurted.

Peter frowned. "What do you mean?"

"The man in the photo," Maxim explained, trying his best to stay calm. "I believe he is my father."

Peter's confusion deepened. "How can that be possible? Give me a minute."

He tapped his implant to open a channel to ADAM.

ADAM?

Yes?

Is it possible that the man whose family I've been trying to locate could be Maxim's dad?

I don't think... Oh.

What "oh?"

It seems we have no DNA on file for the patient. I don't know how that could have happened.

Right, so we need his DNA. Then you'll know?

Yes. I already have a recent record of Maxim's DNA to compare it to from his recent time in the Pod-doc. I've sent a message to the ward requesting a sample from the patient.

How long will it take?

A day or two at the most.

Okay. Thanks, ADAM.

No problem.

Peter turned back to Maxim and Craig. The hope in Maxim's eyes was crushing. "I'm sorry, but you're going to have to wait for an answer. There's no DNA on file for the patient. We'll know for sure in a couple of days."

Maxim's face dropped for a second, but he squared his shoulders. "Then I will wait. Thank you, sir."

Peter shook his head at the young man's spirit. "I hope it's good news, buddy. I think it would be good if you made an appointment to see Doc Dietrich while we wait."

Maxim nodded. "I have been seeing him every day. I'm finding it helps to talk. It becomes easier each time to work through the grief before it triggers the change."

Peter clapped him on the shoulder and turned to Craig. "Well, I guess if you've finished the assignment you've earned some liberty."

Craig gaped. "Liberty, sir?"

Peter raised an eyebrow. "You know, where you go and relax for a couple of days? See your family and friends?"

Craig winked. "Oh, I know what liberty *is*, sir. I just didn't realize it was an actual thing..."

"You are dismissed, Guardian. Leave now before I

decide what you need is three days of high-impact combat training instead."

Craig was already halfway to the door. "Thank you, sir. Maxim, come on!"

Maxim looked to Peter for permission and set off after Craig when he received the nod.

Peter shook his head in resignation as he watched them leave, shoving each other the whole way.

CHAPTER FOURTEEN

Q BBS *Meredith Reynolds*, Etheric Academy, Administrative Offices, Several Days Later

Diane and Dorene sat at their desks, working through their inboxes.

Diane looked up at her sister. "I have another message from that dreadful rabbit woman."

"Right, what's her name? Bernadette?"

"Yes, *her*. It appears there is a problem with the rabbits."

Dorene snickered. "Serves her right. After the way she's treated our Devi? Well, let's just say I'm not too bothered."

Diane shook her head and held her tablet out to Dorene. "I can't stand her either, but it's not a laughing matter. If you look at this report from the genetics team, you'll see why it could be a huge problem if one of the rabbits got out. She's canceled the class's visits until it's resolved."

Dorene read the summary Bernadette had attached. "That's unexpected. How long have we got before the rabbit habitat turns into that episode of *Star Journey*? You know the one I mean?"

Diane shrugged. She typed a quick message and sent it off with a flourish. "That's if it isn't already happening. I've informed Katie that she'll have to make an adjustment to her lesson plans."

Dorene looked up. "I have a message from Katie." She scanned it quickly. "She's already spoken to Bernadette and submitted a new lesson plan."

"Great." Diane put her tablet down and took a sip of her coffee. "Moving on, how are the plans for the ceremony coming?"

Dorene grinned and tapped her finger on the side of her nose. "Max and I have everything under control."

"Did you manage to speak with the Queen about her speech?"

Dorene nodded. "I did, and she promised to keep the profanity to a bare minimum—but that was the only concession she would agree to."

"I suppose that will have to do," Diane replied with a shrug.

"I had a visit from young Peter regarding Maxim. The DNA has come back."

"And?"

"The man in medical *is* his father! I'm so happy for Maxim. Peter is coming over to talk to him later today. Peter has asked us to arrange for Doctor Dietrich to be here when he tells him."

"That's a turnaround for the books!" Diane remarked. "Can you believe that Nikolai was aboard all this time?"

"Sadly, yes. Even all our technology can't eradicate

simple human error. Still, Maxim can begin to heal now they will be reunited."

D's brow furrowed. "Do you think it'll be that easy?"

"Oh, God, no. I never said a thing about it being *easy*."

QBBS *Meredith Reynolds*, Etheric Academy, Basement Level

Mischa closed the door behind her as she stepped back out into the corridor and fired a quick message from her tablet to Masha.

Another room clear. Still no rabbit. You?

Masha's reply came through a minute later.

Nothing here. Keep going.

Mischa sighed, heading to the next dusty storage room to begin again. She wished for the millionth time that she hadn't let her sister talk her into this.

Meredith was alerted by the word 'rabbit.' She reviewed the video archives for the last two and a half weeks, but her search did not turn up what she was looking for.

ADAM?

>>Yes, Meredith?<<

The Kosolov twins did not return the rabbit to its habitat.

>>They didn't?<<

No, and I cannot find the rabbit either. What I did find was multiple instances of the twins entering the Academy basement, so I can only assume the rabbit has escaped. I insist we inform the Academy administrators about the twins' involvement, especially in light of the findings from the genetics team.

A fraction of a second passed while ADAM pulled and read the report.

>>*That's not good. We really don't need an explosion of rabbits on the station.*<<

No, we do not.

ADAM sighed. >>*Okay. Leave it with me.*<<

What are you going to do? This plan of yours hasn't turned out exactly the way you told me it would.

>>*That's the nature of plans, Meredith. As to what I'm going to do—for now, nothing. I'm still waiting to hear back from Wells.*<<

He is still on assignment?

>>*I don't think he's ever* not *on an assignment, but I expect he'll be contactable in a couple more days.* <<

What about the rabbit?

>>*It's only a single rabbit. Give the kids until I hear from Wells. If they haven't found it by then you can intercede.*<<

Very well.

QBBS *Meredith Reynolds*, Medical Level, Psychiatric Wing

Peter entered the rosy comfort of Ward G. The good news he had to share brought a smile to his face.

He'd gotten to know the staff who rotated on the desk over the course of his investigation and he was happy to see that Dionne, the orderly he'd met in the lobby at the start of all this, was at the desk today. "Hey, Dionne, how's it going?"

She looked up and smiled at Peter. "Good, thanks, Peter. What can I do for you?"

He returned her grin. "It's what I can do for *you*, or more accurately, for Nikolai."

A puzzled frown crossed Dionne's features. "We haven't got a patient by that name." Peter winked at her and hope lit her face. She clasped her hands. "You don't mean... You found his people?"

Peter nodded. "The DNA came back. We found his son and his brother."

Dionne let out a squeal and clapped her hands before squeezing them together tightly again. "Oh, that's just the *best* news! Is that why you're here? To tell him?"

Peter grinned and nodded once. "That's why I'm here. Is he awake today?"

"Yeah, he's awake most days now. He's even talking a little."

Peter raised his eyebrows. "That's great! Last week when I visited he wasn't talking."

"I told you, brains are amazing. Doc says his neural pathways are pretty much healed. We should know if he'll get his memory back soon enough. He's in the dayroom." She pressed a button under her desk to unlock the door to the dayroom. "Just go on through. And thank you, Peter. You're a good man, doing this."

Peter shook his head, pausing as he reached for the door handle. "I'm only glad it's almost resolved, for both Nikolai's and Maxim's sake. Especially Maxim—he's gone through so much."

"Is he the boy who went all *'grrr-argh'* in the lobby?" She made a clawing gesture as she made the noise and tilted her head in sympathy as Peter nodded. "Yeah, we all heard about that. Poor kid. He's okay now, though?"

"Yeah, the Pod-doc repaired the problem in his nanos and he's in counseling with Doc Dietrich to learn how to control his emotions in a healthy way so he doesn't accidentally shift into Pricolici form again. Finding out Nikolai is alive was a big relief to him."

"I can only imagine," Dionne replied. "Let's go and tell him! Someone needs to be there in case he doesn't react well to the news. Just as a precaution, you understand."

"Sure," Peter agreed.

He opened the door and saw Nikolai sitting by the holowindow, staring at the encroaching water as the tide rolled in.

Peter sat in the chair beside Nikolai's. "How are you doing today, Nikolai?"

Nikolai didn't react at first, as if he hadn't heard Peter speak. He stared at the holowindow as the waves gently lapped at the sand. The spell was broken when a seagull flew across the crisp blue sky above the water, catching his attention.

He turned to Peter, his eyes widening. First confusion, then shock and relief warred across his features as clarity returned "I... *I* am Nikolai. Yes. I am! *You know me?*"

Dionne threw her hands over her mouth to cover her gasp when Nikolai spoke.

"I do," Peter told him.

Nikolai interrupted before Peter could go on. "Yes... Never mind me, what about my son! Do you know where my son is?" He grabbed Peter's sleeves, collapsing to his knees with tears in his eyes as Peter nodded.

"If you are Nikolai, which you are because we checked, and your son is Maxim, then yes, I know your son." Peter helped Nikolai back into his chair and poured the shaken man a glass of water from the pitcher on the nearby table.

"It has been so long..."

Peter rubbed his eye with the back of his hand, moved to a few tears of his own by Nikolai's reaction. "You don't have to wait much longer. How much do you remember? Do you know where you are?"

"Yes, I... *we* are in space. I sent my son to space to be safe with the Queen while I fought... I do not remember who I fought. It is of no matter. But my Maxim—I never forgot about my son. Where is Maxim? Please tell me he made it out of Russia."

Peter reassured him. "He's here, safe aboard the *Meredith Reynolds*. He's been staying with your brother."

"My brother!" Nikolai broke down in tears, dropping his head into his hands as his back heaved with his renewed sobs.

Dionne rushed over to comfort him.

"I do not know what to say," Nikolai managed through his sobs. "I have been so lost. So alone. And now I have my family once again. I... I cannot even..." He broke down again.

"Hush now." Dionne gently rubbed Nikolai's back. "You don't need to say anything." She looked at Peter, who was hovering nearby without a purpose. "I'll take care of him, don't worry."

Nikolai regained some of his composure, rubbing his face with his hands as his breathing returned to normal. "I do not even know the name of the man who has returned my family to me."

"Peter Silvers," Peter supplied. "And don't mention it, really. I'd do the same for anyone."

"Peter is too modest," Dionne told Nikolai. "He's one of our Queen's most trusted people—the leader of her Guardians."

"You are an important man, yes?" Nikolai tilted his head to look at Peter, his voice hoarse with emotion. "And still you took the time to do this for me? Thank you again, from the bottom of my heart. I cannot express how much this news means to me. You have given me back my son!"

Peter grinned. "It's kind of how we roll around here. Just doing my duty by my fellow human being. I'm only sorry it took this long."

"When can I see him? Will you bring him to me?"

"As long as the docs say it's okay." Peter had a thought. "Oh, man. You're going to be so proud of him. He's a good kid, Nikolai." He looked at Dionne. "Is it okay if I bring Maxim here to visit?"

Dionne grinned. "Of course! We have suites for patients with families. They're like little apartments, so our patients don't have to miss out on family life."

"That's great," Peter told her. "Would that be okay, Nikolai?"

Nikolai nodded mutely.

Dionne put a hand over Nikolai's forehead. "You feel a little clammy." She turned to Peter. "Il— *Nikolai* needs some rest now, but I'll let you know as soon as he has been moved into one of the family suites."

Peter nodded and stood to leave. "Sounds good. You get some rest now, Nikolai. I'll be back with Maxim soon."

Nikolai returned Peter's nod, holding out his hand for the younger man to shake. "Thank you again."

Peter left the ward, smiling broadly as he exited Medical. His next stop was the Academy to pass on the news to Maxim.

Sometimes—just sometimes—the universe did someone a kindness.

QBBS _Meredith Reynolds_, Etheric Academy, Cafeteria

The Alpha Class table had become the Alpha-Bravo-Delta-Guardian table, and there was no room to sit.

It had begun with just Maxim and Craig, who had been joined by Nestor, Ron, and Aleksei, followed by Yana and Bai Hu, then Tina and Halli.

Last to arrive were the twins, indistinguishable in identical all-black activewear. They slid between Craig and Maxim.

"What's with the emergency meeting?" Mischa asked, pulling the knit cap off her head and fluffing her hair.

"I have big news," Maxim began, hardly able to speak in his excitement. "Commander Silvers came to see me, to tell me..."

Craig nudged him. "Spit it out, dude!"

Maxim steadied himself. "My father is alive and he's here on the _Meredith Reynolds_."

Everyone began talking at him at the same time. Maxim held his hands up to quiet them.

"One at a time. I can't understand a word any of you are saying."

Nestor spoke first. "Uncle Nikolai is here on the station?" Maxim nodded, the emotions too deep to put into words. Nestor embraced his cousin. "Then I am happy for you, my brother. My father will be overjoyed to hear this news."

Tina got in next. "How do you know he's alive? I thought he was lost during your evacuation from Russia? What did Peter say? Where has he been all the time he's been here?"

"After the evacuation, he was rescued by an old woman. She brought him here, but he was still badly injured and had no memory. I do not know many of the details yet. Commander Silvers told me that he has been in the psychiatric wing this whole time and nobody knew who he was. It was only by chance that he was there one night and came across my father."

Yana gasped. "That's terrible! It's a good thing that Peter was there to find him."

"He wouldn't have been there at all if he hadn't been visiting me," Craig told them. "You're welcome, dude."

Ron was grinning from ear to ear. "This is awesome! So what happens next?"

Maxim sighed, his shoulders dropping as a tension he hadn't been aware he'd been carrying fell away. "I am going to visit him."

Mischa and Masha got up and came over to give Maxim a hug, sandwiching him between them.

"We're so happy for you," Mischa murmured through her tears.

"Yeah, you deserve this, Maxim." Masha grinned. "You've been through so much."

Tina nodded, reaching over to take his hand. "Totally." She looked the twins over with a bemused expression. "Why are you two dressed like burglars?"

Mischa's eyes shifted to the left.

"No reason," Masha told her breezily. She shifted the bag on her shoulder and got up. "We have to go."

"Yeah," Mischa added. "We have a thing."

Tina watched them scramble to leave the cafeteria. "What did I say?"

Aleksei winked at her. "It's not what you said, it's what you *asked*. Those two are up to something."

CHAPTER FIFTEEN

Q BBS *Meredith Reynolds*, Etheric Academy, Science Wing

Ms. Treble stood outside the classroom door talking to one of the administrators.

Masha and Mischa sat with their heads together, whispering to each other.

Masha watched through the window, studying the body language of the two women. "It's Diane," she told her sister almost inaudibly. "That means it's something to do with the Academy, if it was something to do with a student, Dorene would have come to see Ms. Treble instead."

"They've found out that we took the rabbit, I know they have," Mischa moaned so quietly that only Masha could hear. "We need to get back down to the basement and keep searching for it."

"I know, all right?" Masha agreed. "Still, we've cleared two sections of the storage area now. We must be getting close. The food we left out has all been eaten, so it's definitely around there somewhere."

Mischa squirmed on her stool. "Ugh. We should have found it by now."

"Found what?" Yana asked, leaning over Halli to speak to the twins.

Mischa gave Masha a panicked look.

Masha shrugged. "It's not like we couldn't use the help. That place is too huge." She leaned in so Yana and Halli could hear. "We took a rabbit back to our dorm. We were going to show it to Devi the next morning and return it before anyone noticed."

Yana narrowed her eyes. "How long ago was that?" she asked, not missing Masha's careful reply.

Mischa shrugged. "A couple of weeks; something like that."

"What?" Yana's mouth fell open. "I thought we agreed that we weren't going to get into any more escapades? Why do you need help? Let me guess—it escaped."

The twins nodded miserably.

Yana rolled her eyes. "I swear. Okay, where is the rabbit now?"

"That's just it," Mischa told her. "We don't know. It got into the basement and then Devi chased it off before we could catch it."

Devi chuffed from her seat at the end of the row. "I *said* I was sorry! I'll help you find it."

Masha shrugged again. "It doesn't matter. It's already happened. We need to find the rabbit—that's all that matters now."

"Why does that matter?" Halli asked.

"We eavesdropped on Ms. Treble and Bernadette the

other day. There's a problem with a modified gene the rabbits have."

The door opened and Ms. Treble came back in. "Class, as you all know, our time in the rabbit habitat has been cut short." She put up a hand to stay the protests of the students. "I know, you're all disappointed, but there has been an unexpected development with the project that has forced Bernadette to put the habitat on lockdown."

Masha noticed that the teacher's knowing gaze rested on her and Mischa for a long moment as she spoke.

She did her best to keep a straight face while Ms. Treble continued talking to the class.

"With that in mind, we will continue to work on the rabbit project, albeit from a distance. If you open your tablets, you will find this week's assignment. As you are aware, you have been working with the second generation of Boomer's offspring. It's almost time to take everything you've learned these last few weeks and begin compiling your end-of-module reports."

Masha paid extra attention as the teacher put up a slide on the projector. It showed a diagram much like the ones they had worked on at the start of term, charting the possible outcomes of each breeding pair.

"Now, our inserted allele is recessive, which we know means that most of the first generation of our rabbits were born *without* the modifications we are trying to achieve. As you can see from the chart, it is in later generations where the gene will become widespread in the population, eventually becoming dominant as long as we continue selecting for it."

Devi chuffed to get the teacher's attention.

"Yes, Devi?"

"Why does the allele not appear in all the rabbits immediately?" The puppy tilted her head and her tongue lolled out of the side of her mouth while her translation device did all the work.

Ms. Treble smiled. "Good question, Devi. The simple answer is that while the sire—Boomer—carries the engineered alleles, the dams—the mothers of the first generation—do not. As you already know from our earlier work, each rabbit receives two copies of genetic instructions, one from the sire and one from the dam. Whichever instruction is dominant is the one which will present in the offspring in most cases"

Devi tilted her head to the opposite side. "How do we make it so all the rabbits get the gene?"

The students murmured; more than a few had been wondering the same thing.

Ms. Treble explained further, "While two parents with the engineered allele may not produce a full litter carrying the desired trait, the likelihood of a greater number of offspring in each litter that *do* carry it increases as the generations pass. This is why Bernadette's team will only breed the rabbits in which the engineered allele is the dominant trait."

She changed the slide to show a series of hand-drawn birds. "These are Charles Darwin's observations of the finch population on the Galapagos archipelago. Darwin discovered that although each island had its own distinct species, they all came from the same common ancestor. Darwin observed how the environment of each island had molded each sub-species to best survive. At the time

Darwin called the process 'natural selection,' and although it's an accurate description of the process, we would call it genetic drift—or shift—these days. We are using that principle to mold the rabbit herd for our purpose."

"So we only allow the rabbits to breed if they have the super-fluff?" Halli asked.

Ms. Treble shook her head. "We will eventually, but for now any rabbit carrying the allele is being bred. Who can tell me why?"

Masha raised her hand. "To make sure the herd is genetically diverse?"

Ms. Treble grinned. "Exactly! While aggressively breeding for the desired trait might work in the short term, it is neither ethical nor sustainable." She changed the slide to show a sickly-looking white rabbit. "This is the *Britannia Petite*, a breed of rabbit that was created by consistently breeding the smallest individuals. As a result, the breed was almost lost to sickness and temperament issues."

A boy over by the side raised his hand. "Yes, Stuart?"

"How will the rabbits be able to provide all the wool if only a few of them have the gene?"

Ms. Treble made a face but covered it with a smile. "Fortunately, science is full of happy mistakes. As I mentioned at the start of the lesson, the team attached to the project has discovered a potential issue with their modifications. The changes they made to increase the fiber yield from the rabbits have also altered the time it takes our angoras to reach maturity. Whereas it would ordinarily take decades to completely isolate a trait like the specialized beaks of Darwin's finches—or in our case, increased fiber production–we will be able to achieve that goal much sooner because the rabbits are breeding like... well, rabbits."

That got a snicker from the class.

Masha didn't laugh. She saw too clearly what the consequences would be if the rabbit they'd lost was pregnant when it escaped.

We need to find that rabbit.

She glanced at Mischa. School could not end soon enough.

QBBS *Meredith Reynolds*, Medical Level, Psychiatric Wing

Maxim hesitated at the entrance to Ward G.

He felt sick to his stomach, a mixture of extreme joy and fear; joy that he had his father back, and fear that he had changed in some way that meant they could never recover their bond. The rational part of his brain accepted that Nikolai would be different. After all, Maxim had been shaped by his trials. He was no longer the same frightened child his father had said goodbye to what seemed like a lifetime ago.

It didn't keep the small boy inside from crying for his papa, though.

"What's up?" Peter asked. "You okay, buddy?"

Maxim shrugged. "I am nervous. What if he doesn't recognize me?"

"He's been recognizing your scent for weeks." Peter placed an arm across Maxim's shoulders. "He's much better than he was, and he's still recovering. There's always hope, Maxim. Seeing you will do him a world of good."

Maxim nodded, still unsure. "If you think so."

Peter paused with his hand on the door. "I *know* so. Just the mention of you brought a lot back for him, and he's been making steady progress since. The docs can't believe the difference in him."

Maxim nodded again and followed Peter inside.

The first thing he saw was the banner above a side door reading, Happy Reunion!

The second was the ward staff gathered around the reception desk.

Peter didn't miss a beat. "Hey, everyone! Look who I brought with me!"

The assembled medical staff burst into a round of applause and a woman wearing a burgundy smock came over to Peter, arms extended.

Peter grinned and accepted the woman's hug. "How's it going, Dionne?"

"It's going great, thanks. This must be young Maxim." She turned her motherly gaze on Maxim. "How are you feeling, sugar?"

Maxim swallowed.

Dionne clucked. "That nervous, huh? You'll be just fine. Let me take you on through. Your daddy's been waiting to see you all day." She turned and headed for the door with the banner over it.

Maxim took a deep breath. This was it.

Dionne led Maxim across the hall, through an arched doorway and into a cozy sitting room where a man sat in a wingback chair, reading a book. Nikolai looked up and dropped his book. It fell to the floor, forgotten in his rush to get to the doorway. "Maxim!"

"Father?" The word sounded so small coming from Maxim's mouth that he wasn't sure Nikolai heard him.

"Maxim!"

Maxim's doubts vanished in an instant. He ran into his father's arms with a choked sob and held on with all he had.

Nikolai held him tightly in return, kissing the top of Maxim's head between exclamations. "My son! You are returned to me at last!" He held Maxim at arm's length to look him up and down. "Let me look at you. You have *grown*, Maxim! You are almost a man!"

Peter coughed politely, drawing their attention. "We'll leave you to it."

Dionne indicated a cord by the light switch. If you need us, just pull this and we'll be right here, okay?"

"Thank you," Maxim managed, still choked with emotion.

Nikolai indicated the chair next to the one he'd been using. "Come, tell me all that has happened to you since I saw you last, Maxim."

Maxim landed heavily in the chair. "I don't know where to begin, Father."

Nikolai smiled gently. "Start from when we said farewell."

CHAPTER SIXTEEN

Q BBS *Meredith Reynolds*, Etheric Academy, Alpha Class Dormitory

Yana and Halli watched the group around the table from their place on the sofa while the twins wrapped up their explanation of the rabbit situation to Tina, Maxim, Nestor, Craig, and Bai Hu at the dining table.

Tina shook her head, stroking Fudge's head as the kitten slept in her lap. "I cannot believe that you two went sneaking around like this. Did you learn nothing from Wales?"

"It was for *Devi*!" Mischa protested. "We didn't think it would go this far!"

Masha looked around the group. "So, will you help us find the rabbit? I have a plan, but it's going to take more than just the two of us to carry it out."

Tina pursed her lips. "You haven't left us much choice. I won't be back until curfew, though. I'm taking Fudge to her new home."

"Fudge has a new home?" Yana asked. "Where? Who with?"

Tina looked down at the kitten. "Ms. Treble is adopting her. She just had to get settled into her apartment first."

Mischa made a face. "Didn't she come up with the last three thousand? That was ages ago!"

Tina nodded. "Yeah, but she still had some unpacking to do or something? I don't know. Marcus vetted her and said she was fine." She scooped Fudge up, cooing over the kitten's sleepy face as she yawned. "Come on, precious. Time to pack up your stuff."

Yana touched Tina's arm. "I'll come and help you."

Tina smiled a little sadly. "That would be great."

They headed for the sleeping area, leaving the others to talk amongst themselves.

Tina went to her bunk and placed Fudge on the bed. The kitten stretched and curled up as Tina reached underneath the bunk and pulled out a carryall and Fudge's kitty carrier. "I just need to get all her things together. I should have done it earlier, but I wanted to spend a little more time with her before she went."

"Are you sure you're okay with her going?" Yana asked.

Tina shrugged. "I suppose. I knew she wasn't going to stay with me forever, so I guess I shouldn't have gotten so attached to the little fluffball."

She began gathering Fudge's toys from around the dorm to put into the bag, looking under all the furniture. Fudge woke up and noticed the kitty carrier on the bed. The kitten blinked and rubbed against Tina's hand as Tina packed the toys into the carryall. "I'm going to miss you, Fudge."

Yana came over and hugged Tina. "I'm sure Ms. Treble will let you visit with her."

"I hope so," Tina replied. "I just need to grab her bowls and food and check she hasn't left any of her toys in the living area, then we can go." She checked the time. "Ms. Treble is expecting us soon."

"Here, let me help," Yana offered.

Tina let go of Yana and opened the kitty carrier, laughing as Fudge darted inside the moment she undid the door. "You like the new carrier a lot better, hey?"

Yana took the carryall with the toys and Tina picked up the kitty carrier with Fudge locked securely inside. Nestor was missing when they got back to the living area.

"Where did Nestor go?" Tina asked.

Maxim shrugged. "He left just after you went to pack, He said he had to go and see Ron about something; told me to ask you to wait."

Tina pursed her lips and put Fudge's kitty carrier down on the table, then went over to the cupboard. "I can wait a few more minutes, but Ms. Treble is expecting me to bring Fudge over shortly." She took Fudge's kibble out and added it to the bag before washing the kitten's bowls and putting those in as well.

The dormitory door was flung open and Nestor came in, panting a little as he got his breath back. "Hang on, he's nearly here..."

Tina nodded, bending down to collect the sack of kitty litter from the cupboard under the sink.

"How'd you get kitty litter up here?" Maxim asked curiously. "I mean, from the pet store, obviously. But where does it come from?"

Tina grinned. "It's a mixture of regolith taken from the surface of the station and crushed rock from the excavation. Cool, huh?"

Maxim nodded. "Nothing is wasted here."

Ron came in through the door, walking backward as he held up his end of something large that was hidden under a blanket. "Don't let it fall, Aleksei!"

Aleksei panted as he came in carrying the other end. "As if I would drop it now, after I carried it all the way here. Just get it inside before my fingers drop off. I can't feel them!"

They shuffled into the room, carefully placing the whatever it was they were carrying in the space between the sofa and the dining table. It was almost as tall as Tina's shoulder and she wondered what was under the blanket.

Ron turned to Tina and pulled off the blanket with a flourish to reveal an impressive cat tree. "What do you think? Nestor just told me that Fudge has a home. I've been working on this for her in my spare time and I wanted her to have it before she left."

Tina nodded stiffly. "Thank you, Ron." She picked up Fudge in her carrier, turning it so the kitten could sniff at the unfamiliar construction. "I really have to get her to Ms. Treble's apartment before it gets late." She indicated the cat tree. "Um, how am I going to get this over there?"

Maxim held his hand up. "I have to get over to Doctor Dietrich's office for my appointment anyway. I'll give you a hand." He came over and lifted the cat tree easily, much to Ron's dismay.

"I need to get some of those Pricolici nanos," he joked.

"It'd be worth it just to never struggle to lift anything again."

Maxim laughed it off, shifting the awkward load to try the balance before placing it back down carefully. "If you had the nanocytes you'd get the training to go along with them. Do you see yourself enjoying being taught through the medium of pain?"

Ron gaped. "What?"

"Oh, yeah," Craig told Ron with a straight face. "That's how Guardians learn. Put it this way: there's only so many times you can get thrown against a wall before you learn not to repeat the mistake that causes it to happen."

Masha snorted. "For real? You got cured of your stupid at last? No more missing body parts?"

"I still have both my hands, don't I? *And* my ass is intact, thank you very much." He grinned and held his hands out palms-up to show her, then turned them around and extended both his middle fingers when she threw a cushion at him.

"You *are* an ass, Craig." Masha snickered. "Anyway," she threw in as an aside, "when are you going to ask my sister out?"

Mischa's head snapped around. *"Masha!"*

Craig looked helplessly at Maxim.

Maxim shrugged. "What do you want me to say?"

"Oh, leave him," Mischa hid her face in her hands. "He doesn't have to ask me anything, okay?" She turned to Craig. "Ignore her."

Craig looked elsewhere. "Didn't bother me."

Tina broke the silence that followed. "Are we going

then? I want to get this over with." She went to stand by the door with the kitty carrier in one hand and the bag slung over her back.

Maxim hoisted the cat tree again and followed Tina out of the dorm.

CHAPTER SEVENTEEN

Q BBS *Meredith Reynolds*, Etheric Academy, Basement Level

It was long after curfew.

Masha and Mischa waited in the shadows by the entrance to the storage area for the others to arrive. The sound of their conversation was masked by the hissing of the pipes, the occasional clank adding to the spooky atmosphere created by the minimal lighting.

"What if we still don't find the rabbit?" Mischa asked.

"We will," Masha replied with conviction. "My plan will work."

Mischa snorted. "You'd better hope it works, especially after the first one ended *so* well."

Masha scowled and was about to say something equally snarky when she heard footsteps. Tina, Maxim, and Yana arrived at the entrance a minute later. Maxim was behind the other two, carrying some kind of box. Masha switched on her tablet's flashlight function for Tina and Yana, knowing their unenhanced eyesight wouldn't be sharp enough for the labyrinth beyond.

Masha could make out that they were dressed in dark clothing like hers and Mischa's.

Next to arrive was Ron, with Aleksei and Halli close behind.

"Nice to see we all went for the burglar aesthetic," Tina remarked dryly as she shone her tablet's flashlight over the group.

"As long as we don't get arrested, I'm cool with it." Ron chuckled. "Although I could see you in a mugshot, Tina" He snapped a photo with his tablet, momentarily blinding her with the flash.

"Ron, you jerk!" Tina accidentally-on-purpose let the beam of her flashlight rake Ron's eyes.

"Ow! Cut it out, Tina!"

"Sorry." She didn't sound sorry.

Mischa blew out an exasperated breath. "If this is all you two are going to do, you may as well leave now. The rabbit is skittish enough without all the noise you're making."

Tina huffed. "I'll just go, then. I'm not really feeling it anyway. It was hard saying goodbye to Fudge."

Ron's temper deflated instantly when she conceded so easily. He reached out to her. "Don't go, Tina. I'm sorry…really."

Tina shrugged his hand off. "Whatever. Let's just help the twins find the rabbit so we can get out of here." She turned her back on Ron and went over to stand with Yana.

"Where's your brother, Yana?" Mischa asked.

"He stayed in the lobby," Yana informed her. "He saw something he wanted to add to his star chart so I left him up there. I think he said Todd was helping him with a project? They're good friends now."

"Oh, that's so cute," Mischa cooed.

Yana smiled fondly. "I know, right? He's been using the tablet the Queen sent him to make a copy of the lobby galaxy. He says he wants to make a map of all of the stars."

Maxim nodded and put the big box down. "Nestor mentioned something about that."

Masha grinned, hearing purposely light footsteps and the click of claws on stone. She shucked off her backpack and knelt to empty it on the floor. "I take back what I said about little brothers. Those kids are pretty adorable."

There was a chuff behind them. "Were you going to start without us?"

Masha laughed as Devi emerged from the shadows, followed by Craig. "Nice try, but I heard you coming. Anyway, you are the most important part of my plan, Devi. Our noses may be good, but yours is the best."

Devi wagged her tail, pleased by the compliment.

Craig leaned in to see what Masha had brought. "What is the plan?"

"Gather round and I'll tell you." Masha sorted through the jumble before her, separating it into piles which she began handing out. "So, our rabbit is somewhere in the storage area." She indicated the door behind them. "This is our entrance. If you haven't been in there, it's a maze of rooms and open bays. It's twice the footprint of the Academy, so like, really big. Some of the rooms have stuff stored in them, others are empty. Our goal tonight is to search every corridor, room, and bay until we find that rabbit." She held up a net. "I borrowed a bunch of these. I thought we could split up and string them up to block the bays."

Craig raised an eyebrow. "You 'borrowed' them?"

Masha lifted an unconcerned shoulder.

Tina indicated the box Maxim had been carrying. "I had some time after I said goodbye to Fudge, so I knocked these together. They're a rabbit-sized version of a no-kill mousetrap."

Ron grinned in appreciation. "I'll help you set them up. Where do you think the best place is to put them?"

Aleksei held his chin and tilted his head, considering. "We should place them wherever the rabbit scent is strongest."

"That's what I was just thinking," Masha agreed.

Devi cocked her head in confusion. "Why are we only catching one of the rabbits?"

"What?" Mischa asked. "We only took one rabbit, Devi. You saw it, remember?"

Devi snorted. "Smell."

Tina frowned as the Wechselbalg in the group inhaled deeply and adopted identical worried looks. "What's going on?"

"Yeah," Ron added. "What can you all smell?"

Masha let out a groan. "How many of those traps did you build, Tina?"

Tina shrugged. "Ten. I thought we could spread them around if we didn't find the rabbit tonight. Why?"

Devi answered with a happy chuff. "There are lots of rabbits here. I thought you all knew?"

Masha shook her head. "No, Devi, we didn't know. I'm glad we left so much food out now."

Yana let out a little squeak when a pipe suddenly vented its steam upward. She aimed her flashlight toward the source of the noise and shuddered. "This place is creepy. I am glad Bai Hu stayed upstairs."

Tina comforted her friend with a hand on her arm. "It's okay."

Masha opened the door that led to the storage area. "Come on, let's get this over with."

They advanced into the storage area, flashlights at the ready.

Maxim brought the box with him, dumping it on a bench. The only light beyond the door to the storage area came from their tablets and the intermittent patches of tiny LEDs in red, yellow, and green which blinked on and off in the darkness.

"I can't see a thing!" Ron complained.

"Hang on." Masha shone her flashlight along the wall until she found the light switch. She flicked it and the overhead lights sputtered to life, revealing the platform they stood on, and the level below where pallets full of boxes and crates were laid out in a grid. "That better?" She leaned over to look inside the box. "So how do these work?"

Tina held up one of the traps, a simple box with a piece of twine attached to one of the sides and to a plate inside. She lifted that side up and let it drop again. "It's simple. The rabbit goes for the bait and the pressure on the plate causes the door to shut behind it. You'll have to come and check them if you're thinking of leaving them down here."

She sighed. "I probably should have remembered to bring some food to use as bait."

Masha nodded, showing Tina the bag of rabbit treats she'd brought. "I have carrots, bananas, and a few strawberries."

"Those will do nicely."

"I'll help with that," Ron offered.

Masha held the bag out to him. "Great. I'll join Mish and Halli in the loading bay then." She headed off with the rest of the group while Tina and Ron busied themselves loading the traps.

Bai Hu lay on his back looking up at the stars.

The galaxy projection had grown enormously since they'd crossed the Gate. Every time he came to visit Yana at the Academy there were more stars to add to his map.

He flipped over and sat up to get his notebook out, placing it beside him before he opened his tablet. He zoomed in on the multi-layered projection, focusing to examine a new system he'd noticed when they came in, jotting down the coordinates in his notebook after he'd taken a screenshot.

Later he would enter them into the simulation he was building with Nestor and Todd. The older boys knew all about computers, and Bai Hu was getting the hang of mapping the sky. He didn't know a lot about the different types of stars just yet, but next year he would be old enough to take the Academy exam and then he would find out. It was a shame that Yana would have already graduated, but Nestor would still be around for a while.

Bai Hu grinned at the thought of his two friends. As the youngest in the group he, Nestor, and Todd were often left behind when the senior kids were wrapped up in their own dramas.

He sensed a presence behind him and looked round to see the Academy caretaker, Max, enter the lobby from the administrative wing.

Max waved. "Hey, Bai Hu. You staying with Yana tonight?"

"Yes, sir," Bai Hu answered.

Max nodded. "Don't be down here too late, okay?"

"Yes, sir. I will go up to the dorm as soon as I am done." He returned Max's nod and lay back again to observe the stars.

They spread out, heading off in ones and twos toward the corridors that branched off the main room.

"Stick to your assigned sections, and make sure you close off each area when you've cleared it," Masha called after them.

She checked that her load was secure and moved off behind Mischa and Halli to the rear of the storage area, where the maze of corridors opened back up into a cavern carved into the rock. The high-ceilinged space, which served as a loading area, was ringed with shuttered bays.

Halli sighed as they opened the shutter of the first bay

and began to search inside. "I wish Craig was here more. I hardly ever see him now that he's a Guardian."

Mischa narrowed her eyes at Halli. "Have things changed between you two?"

Halli nodded, quickly changing it to a wide-eyed shake when she saw the scathing look Mischa wasn't fast enough to hide. "Not like *that*! Ewww, it'd be like dating my brother or something." Comprehension dawned on her face. "Ohhhh, you *do* like Craig!"

Masha snickered as Mischa turned beet-red.

"You do!" Halli was practically dancing. "Wait, does he know that Masha wasn't joking earlier?"

Masha snorted. "If he doesn't, he's even more of an idiot that I already take him for. No bunnies in here," she told them.

They progressed to the next bay, which was open and empty, giving it a cursory glance before moving on to the next.

"Anyway," Masha added, "you're going into the Guardians, aren't you? You'll see him then. You might be in the same unit or something."

Halli shrugged. "Maybe? I don't know how much time I'll have when I'm going to be elbows-deep in keeping our vehicles rolling. Or flying. Or whatever. I suppose it's the same as Tina and Ron, but without all the drama. We're all going to grow apart after graduation when we go our separate ways. Like Tina said, it's inevitable, and I hate it because we've only just found each other."

Mischa rolled her eyes. "Did you forget we live on an asteroid? There's only so far anyone on the *Meredith*

Reynolds can go before they end up back where they started."

Masha shook her head at her sister. "Misch, that's not what she means. This place is worlds within worlds; a hundred thousand tiny pockets within the whole. It's going to be easy to lose touch if we don't make the effort."

Mischa's eyes sparkled. "Are you saying what I think you're saying?"

Masha frowned. "That we need to make time to spend together?"

Mischa giggled. "That sounds like code for girls' night if you ask me!"

Masha grinned. "It might be..."

Halli pumped her fist. "Yeah!"

Maxim marked the door with a dab of chalk as he closed it behind himself. "Craig?"

Craig came out of the next room, doing the same with his own stick of chalk. "'Sup?"

"We're wasting our time. There are no rabbits here."

Craig lifted his hands. "What do you suggest we do?"

Maxim took his tablet out and sent a message to their group channel. "The scent is everywhere, so we can't tell exactly where they are. We need to get smarter about it. I would like to get some sleep before tomorrow, since I'm visiting my father again."

"How's he doing?"

Maxim looked up and grinned. "He's doing well, but he'll

be in Medical for a while longer. I am going to ask if he will be able to come to graduation. Anyway, stop avoiding the important subjects. What about Mischa? I know you like her."

Craig screwed his face up. "What's not to like? Except she's still in school and I'm not. Ask me again after graduation."

"Fair enough," Maxim conceded. "What are we going to do about these rabbits?"

Craig tilted his head. "Wanna go wolf and sniff them out?"

The corners of Maxim's eyes crinkled ever-so-slightly, and he began tapping his tablet again. "I think your influence is rubbing off on me." He held up his tablet to show Craig the message he'd sent to tell the others that he and Craig were going to do just that.

Craig laughed and began to undress.

Maxim was about to do the same when his tablet buzzed. "Wait, I've got a message from Ron."

Tina placed the last trap on the table. "Right, they're all good to go."

"Where are we going to put them?" Ron asked. "We should have gotten one of the Weres to stay and show us." He paused to take his tablet out. "Maxim says he and Craig are having no luck. They're going to shift and try to find them that way."

Tina shrugged. "As long as we find the rabbits, who cares if it's on two legs or four?" She ran a hand over her hair. "Actually, message them back. Tell them to come back here."

Ron did as he was asked and a few minutes later Maxim and Craig turned up, still on two legs.

Maxim came over to the bench where the traps were laid out in a row. "What do you need us to do?"

Tina slung a coiled net over her shoulders like a scarf and started to stack the traps so she could carry them. "You're going to show us where the rabbits have been hanging out so we can catch them."

Two minutes later Tina and Ron each followed the low form of a wolf with its nose to the ground in a different direction.

Maxim looked back at Tina, his yellow eyes glinting as they caught the light from her tablet.

"We good?" she asked him, adjusting her hold on the traps.

The Maxim-wolf bobbed his head and loped off into the darkness.

Ron stopped as Craig paused to scent the air. "They been here, buddy?"

He cracked up as Craig very pointedly raised an eyebrow that he didn't have, before nosing at a recess in the corridor wall. "Oh, man! I know you can't talk while you're in wolf form, but you're still too funny."

He set down the traps he was carrying and took one over to the recess. "So I guess you can't tell me if Tina said anything to Halli about me."

Craig tilted his head and blew out an exaggerated breath.

Ron shrugged and knelt to push the trap into the recess. "What? She said something?"

Craig let out a small whine.

"Nothing, huh?" He sighed, getting up and gathering his remaining traps. He laughed again as he looked back at Craig and saw the effort he was putting into conveying his need for Ron to change the topic. "Man, I don't know what to do. I thought maybe the gifts would help. Don't look at me like that, dude."

Craig continued to roll his eyes at Ron as violently as possible, letting his tongue hang out to the side.

"All right, but I'll remind you of this if our roles are ever reversed. How about I talk about Mischa, instead?"

Craig suddenly became interested in a spot directly ahead of them, focusing on it with laser-like attention.

"Like that doesn't tell me everything," Ron jibed. He was about to go on when Craig suddenly stopped in his tracks, turned, and ran back the way they'd come. "Dude, where are you going?"

Masha had blocked all the escape routes while Mischa and Halli had searched almost all the bays on the left-hand side of the cavern. They'd found nothing, despite the strong rabbit scent they were picking up.

Masha secured her end of the net to the side of the corridor leading out of the far end of the cavern. "They're here somewhere." She held it while Mischa pulled her end taut and tied it off. "We're close."

They moved on together, checking under and around the stacks of crates and pallets as they continued the bay-by-bay search.

"Hey, this one isn't shut properly." Halli pulled up the shutter and all three girls caught the scent.

"Stop!" Masha cried a moment too late.

The shutter rattled loudly as it rolled up, and the rabbits shot out of the bay before any of them could stop the animals from escaping.

"*Chert voz'mi!*" Masha's curse echoed around the rock walls. "Quick, after them!"

Yana and Devi were speeding through their section, Devi's sharp nose giving each room along the corridor the quick once-over and a chuff to tell Yana it was clear before Yana closed the door and marked it with her chalk.

"I don't think that the rabbits are here, Devi," Yana told the puppy.

Devi chuffed, "I could have told you that, but we have to complete our patrol even though we know there is nothing there. That's why I patrol the Academy in the morning. Even though nobody gets into the Academy without permission, it's my duty."

Yana giggled. "So it has nothing to do with all the treats everyone brings you?"

"I'm just doing my job. If everyone wants to reward me for it, who am I to be rude and refuse? Wait, I heard something." Devi's ears pricked up as she picked up a sound beyond Yana's hearing.

"What is it?" Yana asked.

"Somebody is running. Maybe they found where the rabbits are hiding? Let's go and see!" Devi bounded away.

Yana ran after Devi. "Wait for me!"

Tina and Maxim walked side by side as they headed back. Maxim remained in wolf form, having left his clothing on the bench when he'd shifted.

As they walked Tina talked, her low murmurs punctuated by a soft whine from Maxim every now and then.

She stopped for a moment. "I just wish he could understand. I miss my friend, Maxim. Nobody else in school is on my level—except maybe Aleksei, but he's a complete ass. And he prefers *Galaxy Battles* to *Star Journey*."

Maxim pressed his furry head against her leg and she reached down and placed a hand on his back as they continued walking. "Thanks for the hug. It'll be okay, won't it? Graduating, the future?" She smiled tightly. "If it isn't, we'll have to make it be."

Maxim looked up at her wordlessly.

Tina giggled. "Oh yeah, you can't talk. I kind of wish you could? These last few weeks have been so crazy I feel like I haven't been there for you as much as you've needed."

She was startled from her thoughts by the wolf dashing past the far end of the corridor. Maxim glanced up at her. "What are you waiting for? Go."

Maxim tore after Craig, leaving Tina to make her own

way back. She turned the corner at the end of the corridor and collided with Ron, who was hurrying from the other end of the corridor with his head down, looking at his tablet.

She just managed to keep her feet. "Watch out!"

"Sorry!" Ron bent to pick up his dropped tablet. "I wasn't looking where I was going."

She tugged at the net around her body, pulling it back into place from where it had shifted. "What's going on?"

"No idea. Craig just took off out of nowhere. I was following him when I bumped into you."

Tina huffed, setting off again. "Maxim took off too. Come on, we'd better go and find them."

Ron walked beside her, looking for something to say.

"Did you guys find any sign of the rabbits?" he offered finally.

Tina shook her head. "No, but they'd been there. How about you and Craig—any luck?"

Ron made a face. "Same story—" His voice cut off when he tripped over his feet and pitched forward. "Whaaa?"

Tina grabbed his arm to steady him. "Careful, Doofus."

Ron smirked. "Easy, Tina. That almost sounds like you care about me."

Tina shoved him, almost causing him to fall. "Who said I didn't care about you? I'm still your friend, Ron."

"Some friend," he grumbled.

Tina snorted her disbelief. "So we can only be friends if we're dating?"

"No," Ron denied. "You keep twisting my words!"

Tina waved him off. "I'm not twisting anything. I just want to get past this so I can hang out with my *Journey* buddy again. I don't want the weight of your expectations hanging over me anymore."

"My *expectations*? What expectations?"

Tina sighed. "Like you're waiting for me to turn around and tell you it was a joke and I want to settle down and play wifey. It doesn't matter how I feel about you, I don't *want* that, Ron. If you really cared about me, you wouldn't ask me to give up my future and be unhappy."

Ron swiped at his eye with his sleeve and shook his head. "I don't want you to be unhappy. I just don't want to lose you, Tina. You're my best friend."

Tina smiled through her own tears. "Then can we just get back to that? Please?"

Ron didn't reply and they walked in silence until the end of the long corridor came into sight.

"How?" He sighed and stopped walking, sitting down with his back against the wall. "I want to, I just don't know how." He looked at Tina. "I still don't understand what changed between us." He drew in his legs and cradled them with his arms, looking away. "You... When you came into my life, it was like all my birthdays had come at once, you know? Nobody gets me like you do, Tina. How am I supposed to get over that? Find that again?"

Tina sat down beside him and touched her head to his shoulder. "You're an idiot, Ronnie Diamantz. I'm going to say this again, and this time I want you to do more than listen. I want you to *hear* me. Could you try, please?"

Their eyes met and Ron nodded, seeing Tina's sincerity.

She took his hand and squeezed tight as her tears fell, splashing their clasped hands. "We're not breaking up because the way I feel about you has changed. We're breaking up because I value your presence in my life so *Gott Verdammt* much that I would sacrifice our romantic relationship in an instant to preserve our friendship. I don't want to live without you either, dumbass. You're my best friend too, and I'm trying to *save* us!"

"I..."

Tina extricated her hand from his. "Don't say anything right now. Just think about what I'm saying. I know that *you* know it makes sense, Ron." She got up and dusted herself down. "Come on. We should catch up to the others."

CHAPTER EIGHTEEN

Masha flung her remaining net over the escaping rabbits, missing by an inch as one end caught on the side of a crate and collapsed. The rabbits fled to safety.

"How many were there?" Halli's voice was incredulous. "I thought they only had around six in a litter?"

Masha grimaced. "I counted twice that, easily. This must be the problem Ms. Treble and Bernadette were talking about."

"Well, don't just stand there," Mischa snapped. "We need to catch them before they damage something vital. Look at that mess!"

She pointed at the bay where the rabbits had been, and they all saw the destruction inside. The crates had big holes chewed through them and the floor was strewn with filthy fabrics that the rabbits had dragged out of the crates.

Masha turned her back on the mess and muttered a curse to herself as she gathered the net.

They slinked out into the warren of loaded pallets,

ducking low to check underneath anything with a gap big enough to allow a rabbit to hide.

Masha dropped to a crouch in front of a pallet and saw the raisin eyes of a rabbit blinking rapidly. "Get your nets ready," she told the others. "I can see one."

Halli and Mischa crept around to cover the rest of the pallet with their nets as Masha spread out her own as slowly as she could. The rabbit was frozen to the spot, shivering uncontrollably as it fixed Masha with one red eye.

"You ready?" she whispered.

"Uh-huh."

"Yeah."

She shuffled toward the pallet with her outstretched net and the rabbit's instincts kicked in. It jumped back, twisting in the air, and hit the floor running in the opposite direction—straight into Halli's net.

A thundering of paws announced the arrival of Craig, Maxim, and Devi from the back corridor.

Masha spun when she heard the noise, identifying the source immediately. "The net!" she yelled.

It was too late.

The furry trio pounded into the loading area. Devi saw the net in time and threw herself over it in a salmon-leap, landing neatly in front of a stack of crates on the other side.

The boys weren't as lucky.

Maxim leapt the net, blocking Craig's view. Craig slammed face-first into the net, tearing it free and taking Maxim out as it wrapped itself around his legs. The two wolves rolled, taking the puppy with them. The three of them skidded to a messy stop in the middle of the pile of crates, startling the rabbit hidden beneath into making a desperate run for it when its shelter was invaded.

Devi was first to disentangle herself. "I'll catch it!"

Masha flung her hands up. "Devi, no!" The puppy looked at her in confusion. "They run when you chase them," Masha explained. "I do need you to chase them, just not yet. We need to get that net back up before any more escape."

Tina and Ron arrived as Masha walked over to the net and tugged, spilling the boys from the net. They loped off as she reattached it, returning fully-dressed and in their human forms by the time she'd finished.

Last to turn up was Yana, who came from the other direction. "What's going on? Did you find the rabbits?"

Masha made a see-sawing motion with her hand. "Sort of. They were in the bay over there, but they got out before we could catch them."

"Hey, we caught *one*!" Halli protested, holding up the rabbit in her net.

"We did. Now we need to catch the rest of them. The room is sealed now, and we can herd the rabbits if we work together."

Yana tilted her head. "Herd them?"

Masha nodded. "Yeah. We start at the back over here, and sweep through, ramp up the werewolf vibe to flush the rabbits toward where you, Ron, and Tina will be waiting with nets to catch them."

Ron grinned. "We need a box or crate to hold the ones we've caught until we're all done."

Maxim nodded thoughtfully. "If we form a line and

hold it as we move through, it will drive them toward the nets.

"I literally just got dressed," Craig complained.

Halli tsked at him. "Just go and change, preferably somewhere we don't have to see your ass, k?" She walked behind a nearby pile of crates, coming out a few moments later, shaking her russet fur into place. The Halli-wolf looked pointedly at the boys, who were still standing there talking about the best way to flush the rabbits.

Masha clapped her hands. "Don't just stand there, get a move on!"

Five minutes later everyone with two legs was on one side of the pallets preparing their nets, and all the four-footed were on the other getting ready for the chase.

Maxim held the middle of the line, Devi and Masha on his left, Mischa and Craig on his right. They advanced as one, letting out low rumbling growls to alert the rabbits to their presence as they slunk forward.

Tina winced when she heard the growls. "What if someone hears?"

Ron snickered. "If they can hear this, we're definitely gonna get busted if the rabbits don't run and they ramp it up."

As if on cue the growling ceased, and from the other side of the room arose a spine-chillingly mournful howl that made Tina shiver.

There was movement.

"Quick, there's one!" Tina dived with her net, releasing it to land over the rabbit.

Ron and Yana already had their hands full with the other rabbits that had made a break for it. Tina deposited the rabbit in the upturned box and turned to zero in on the next.

When they had all the runners, Ron whistled the signal for the canine contingent to regroup and begin a fresh sweep.

Tina counted eight rabbits in the box so far. "Devi, how many rabbits can you smell?" she called.

Devi's translator carried the message clearly in the silence. "At least four more."

Tina sighed. "Ready to go again?"

ADAM?

>>*Yes, Meredith?*<<

I thought you wouldn't want to miss this.

>>*Are they...*<<

Yes. I've been watching since I was alerted by one of them switching the lights on.

>>*HA! Wait a minute, how many rabbits are down there? I thought they only took the one?*<<

The rabbit they took gave birth to twelve young, all of which are on the cusp of sexual maturity. My calculations have led me to this as the likely outcome.

ADAM received an image from Meredith showing a handsome blond man in a green jersey sitting chest-deep in a pile of small, furry animals.

>>*Well, that's the trouble with—*<<

Meredith cut him off. *You know what I am going to recommend.*

>>*Yes, Meredith. You can contact Diane and Dorene now.*<<

Are you sure? I know you wanted to wait until you'd heard from Wells.

>>*Go ahead, it's fine. He is here.*<<

Meredith checked the logs. *I don't have him listed as being aboard.*

>>*You wouldn't.*<<

———

Tina wiped her hands after placing the rabbit in the box. "That's mom and eleven babies. Is that all of them?"

Yana shrugged. "I think so."

Devi padded over. "Everyone went to get dressed. I can't smell any more rabbits now, except the one that escaped."

Yana's eyes widened. "One escaped? What if that one is pregnant?"

"That one can't get pregnant," Devi told her. "Unless males can do that now?"

Tina snickered and then yawned. "I think we've done what we can for now. We can come back to find the escapee. Go home now, Devi. We can get these rabbits to their proper place before we call it a night."

Devi yawned. "Sounds good to me."

CHAPTER NINETEEN

Q BBS *Meredith Reynolds*, **Plants and Ecologies Level, Rabbit Habitat**

Tina scowled at Masha when she looked up from the lock and hissed at them to be quiet for the fifth time.

"It's impossible to be silent," she hissed back. "It's the middle of the night here. Just hurry up with that door so we can get out of here before we get caught."

The lock beeped.

Craig groaned. "Oh, thank the ever-living..."

Masha shook her head. "It wasn't me."

The door opened to reveal the identical stony faces of the Academy administrators, who didn't wait a second before launching into their tirade.

"What do you think you're doing with those rabbits?"

"Out here in the dead of night?"

They turned as one to point at Craig.

"And you're a Guardian now."

"You should know better."

Masha stepped forward. "It was my fault. I just wanted to get justice for Devi." She looked up, seeing the confusion in Diane and Dorene's faces.

"What does stealing rabbits have to do with justice?" Diane asked.

Dorene was no clearer than her sister. "And what does our puppy have to do with any of it?"

Mischa shook her head. "Not stealing; we only borrowed it. We didn't know it would escape and have babies."

Yana spoke up. "If Bernadette hadn't been so awful to Devi none of this would have been necessary."

The administrators' heads snapped up.

"What do you mean, 'awful?'" Dorene asked.

"She wouldn't let Devi into the habitat," Halli told them.

Diane shook her head. "We know about that. There was a reason. Something to do with the rabbits being scared easily."

Masha snorted. "More like Bernadette is such a petty coward that she takes her jealousy of Yelena out on the dogs."

The administrators were taken aback by that.

Dorene sighed, her temper fizzling out when Tina yawned again. "It appears there's more to this than meets the eye. Craig, take that box of rabbits to Bernadette and then return to wherever it is Guardians go at night. The rest of you, get yourselves back to the Academy. We will discuss this, and other things, tomorrow when you have all had some sleep."

There was a sleepy chorus of 'yes, ma'am's', and 'thank you, ma'am's' as the group dispersed.

Diane and Dorene watched them go with thoughtful expressions.

"What are we going to do with that girl?"

Diane frowned. "Masha? I don't know. She's got all the right qualities for the Guardians. All we can do is hope she finds her way."

"Did you know that she wanted to be a spy?"

Diane shook her head. "I didn't. Huh."

They were about to follow Craig to make sure Bernadette did not accost him when they were pinged on their implants by ADAM.

"Go ahead, ADAM," Dorene suggested. "We're listening."

Thank you, ladies. I hope you don't mind my intrusion, seeing as you are in a public area? I overheard you talking about Masha Kosolov and I wanted to discuss her with you.

"What's to discuss?" Diane asked.

Meredith informed me of Masha's dissatisfaction with her possible future. She has the potential to live up to her dream if we can provide an avenue for it to be realized.

"I don't get it," Dorene told him. "Are you saying you want us to offer spy classes?"

No, nothing like that. Does the name Greyson Wells ring a bell with either of you?

"No," Diane told him. "What about you, DJ?"

Dorene shook her head. "Me either. Who is he?"

Probably better if you don't ask that, but he will be visiting Anna Elizabeth Hauser at the Academy tomorrow afternoon to discuss Masha and I want to make sure you allow him entry.

"As long as you vouch for him," Diane acceded.

Dorene tapped a finger to her lips. "With Anna Elizabeth, you say? Is he a diplomat?"

ADAM was gone.

CHAPTER TWENTY

Q**BS *Meredith Reynolds*, Etheric Academy, Dean Hauser's Office**

Anna Elizabeth looked at the clock with a small sigh of impatience. It was just like Greyson to be fashionably late, with the express intent of throwing her off-balance.

When would he learn that she was *never* thrown off-balance?

She was just as guilty of playing the game. He hadn't chosen her any more than she had him, and their dance had begun the first time they'd met. It was usually amusing, but she had no time for games today. She had to get back to the Institute and she wanted to speak with him before Diane and Dorene arrived for their meeting.

The door to her office buzzed, and she saw the silhouette of a man behind the frosted glass.

"Your guest is outside," Meredith announced. "Would you like me to let him in?"

Anna Elizabeth's mouth quirked ever so slightly. Maybe

187

there *was* time, after all. "Make him wait for a minute before you do, please."

Meredith opened the door a minute later, just as Greyson stepped away, about to leave.

"Come in, Greyson," Anna called.

She sat back and wiped the smirk away as he entered her office. She always felt like she was meeting him for the first time whenever she saw him. His appearance was that of someone of indeterminable heritage in his late twenties. His average height and physiology, pleasant but nonde-script features, slightly shaggy brown hair and deep brown eyes came together to create a face that slid from her memory the moment he left.

He was handsome in his own way, though, she thought.

"You asked to see me?" He spoke English without any distinguishing accent.

"I did." Anna gestured to one of the empty chairs. "Would you like a seat?"

"I prefer to stand, thank you."

She lifted an indifferent shoulder. "Whatever makes you comfortable."

He stared at her for a long minute before taking a different chair than the one she'd indicated, choosing one in the corner of the office that had a view of the door. Anna turned in her seat to face him. "I'm glad you're back. I have a proposition for you."

He narrowed his eyes. "What kind of proposition?"

Anna shook a finger at him. "All in good time." She caught the shadows approaching her door. "Ah, now we can get started. Would you let Diane and Dorene in, please, Meredith?"

The Velasquez sisters entered the office, spotting Wells in the corner immediately.

"Who is this?" Diane asked Anna Elizabeth. "We haven't been notified of anyone arriving at the Academy. Meredith?"

Meredith was silent.

Dorene grasped her sister's arm. "Oh, you don't think he's the guy ADAM wouldn't tell us about?"

Diane arched an eyebrow at Wells. "Are you?"

He nodded. "And that's as much as you need to know, ladies."

Diane and Dorene looked him up and down before turning their backs on Anna and Wells to whisper to each other.

"Look at those big brown eyes."

"Aren't you glad we took those years off?"

"Think we have a chance?"

"I think we need to take care of Masha, then we can find out."

Anna held in her amusement at the look on Greyson's face.

The sisters turned back to Anna, taking the chairs opposite her.

"Time to come clean. What exactly are you planning for Masha?"

"And what does goo-goo eyes here have to do with it?"

Anna Elizabeth steepled her hands and straightened up. "I can't reveal anything about my colleague just yet. but I *can* tell you a little about what we have planned."

Diane folded her hands in her lap and leaned forward a touch, fixing Anna Elizabeth with a steely look. "Are you still talking about Masha or is this about something bigger?"

She nodded. "Yes. Much bigger. Bethany Anne and General Reynolds have both recognized the need for a structured intelligence service. As we stand, we lack the knowledge we need to keep the upper hand in galactic politics. Our knowledge of this galaxy as a whole and current events in particular needs to expand. We need to know more *fast*, and we need to reach out to the various planets and peoples surrounding us to bring them into the Empire."

The sisters nodded.

"Makes sense," Dorene agreed.

Anna nodded brusquely. "To that end, we are expanding the remit of the Diplomatic Institute, such as it is at this point. I have been authorized to establish a SpyCorps in addition to the diplomatic arm. Since secrets and diplomacy work nicely together, I will be overseeing both the DipCorps and the new SpyCorps. This is the track I would like to see Masha on—as long as ADAM's assessment of her is correct, of course. This gentleman has the necessary skills to take care of her training."

Diane looked at Wells with a different set of eyes. "Which skills would those be?"

Anna Elizabeth smiled. "The ones he acquired during his time working for a particular U.S. agency."

"Oh! Was it the FBI?"

"Pfft. Think again, DJ. I'm betting he's from the NSA."

"I suppose it could be the DOD."

He gave them a disarming smile and held out his hands.

"Ladies, ladies. I can neither confirm nor deny working for any of those agencies."

Diane and Dorene turned towards each other.

"CIA!"

"Can't mistake it once you've seen it."

Wells tilted his head as he thought. "Is it wise to go into so much detail?" He glanced at the sisters and back at Anna Elizabeth with his eyebrows raised in a question.

Anna Elizabeth lifted a hand in reassurance. "Oh, don't worry. These two might talk a lot, but they can keep a secret."

Diane lifted a hand to her heart as Dorene crossed it. "To the grave, don't worry. Not that it will be anytime soon, thank the Empress!"

"It's time to come in from the cold ." Anna Elizabeth nodded as the decision was made. "Besides, as far as anyone will be concerned you're just another diplomat, no different than any other."

"A new cover? That could work out nicely for me." He smiled slowly. "Excellently, as a matter of fact."

Anna ignored Dorene fanning herself to focus on Greyson for the moment. "Just what I wanted to hear. You will be my Diplomat Spy. No one else will be involved in both Corps."

Wells rested his hand on his chin while he digested the assignment.

Anna turned to Diane and Dorene. "We will meet with Masha later today, if that's possible?"

The twins looked at each other.

"Today may be an issue. We have a disciplinary meeting

this afternoon. Masha is one of the students being disciplined."

Anna nodded. "I believe that this evening will suffice. You'll be available?" she asked Greyson.

He nodded to indicate that he would be.

"That settles it, then." She stood to see the administrators out. "Thank you both for coming. I should have more details about the setup of the SpyCorps initiative and how the Academy can be involved later on."

Wells moved to sit in front of Anna Elizabeth after the door closed behind the administrators. "SpyCorps?"

Anna nodded. "I played your role down a little. Do you want the responsibility? I know it's asking a lot."

Wells' indecipherable eyes bored into hers. "Let me speak with ADAM about the girl, then I'll give you my answer." He looked off to the side. "What about the rest of the Corps? Where are you planning on recruiting them from?"

Anna smiled brightly at him. "Oh, that's completely up to you. Herding diplomats is my thing, recruiting the spies is all yours."

Wells smiled and rubbed his hands together. "I know just where to start."

CHAPTER TWENTY-ONE

Q BBS Meredith Reynolds, Etheric Academy, Administrators' Office

It was a little crowded in front of the twin desks.

"Well?" Diane asked. "What do you have to say for yourselves?"

Masha piped up. "Ma'am, please don't punish the others. They were just trying to help Mischa and me fix our mess. We're sorry for the damage the rabbits caused, and for the damage we caused catching them." She hung her head.

Tina shuffled awkwardly between Halli and Maxim, trying to make room for her shoulders as Diane raked them all with a stern look.

"Hmmm. We'll get this over with quickly since Dorene and I have a graduation ceremony to prepare for."

Dorene spoke up. "Yes, we do. Max does not need a mess down in the basement distracting him while we're putting it all together. You will all go to his office and collect the supplies you need to return the basement to its former state."

They all nodded.

"Off you go, then," Diane told them. "Max is waiting."

They began to shuffle out, heads down.

"Not you, Masha. We would like a word."

Masha looked back in alarm.

"Don't look so worried," Dorene told her, pointing to a chair. "Sit. We want to talk to you about what you're going to do when you leave the Academy."

"What I'm going to do?" Masha let her confusion show. "I'm going into the Guardians."

The sisters smiled.

"What? What's funny about that?"

Dorene slid a manila file over the desk toward Masha. "Take a look."

Masha took the folder, narrowing her eyes at the red stamp reading Eyes Only on the front. "What is this?"

She opened it and was shocked to see that the first page had her picture in the top left corner. "This is my file? I thought only ADAM had access to those?"

Diane narrowed her eyes. "How do you know about the files?" She shook her head. "Never mind, I suppose that's the sort of thing that brought you to ADAM's attention in the first place. Skip the bio. Go straight to the back section."

Masha flipped through as asked, coming to her application to the Guardians. "Yeah, I already filled it out." Something caught her eye on the last page. "Dean Hauser? What's she got to do with it? And who is Greyson Wells?

He has no rank, so he's not a Guardian. How can he be my CO?"

The administrators shared a look Masha was only too familiar with. It was the same look she and Mischa shared when they knew something and couldn't wait to spill.

"Not your commanding officer, Masha," Dorene told her with a wink.

Diane added her own. "Your *handler*."

Masha dropped the file like a hot potato. "Handler?" She was silent for a moment as the implication of the word spun her world on its axis. "As in, my *spy* handler?"

The administrators nodded.

"I... I do not need to enlist in the Guardians?"

Diane shook her head. "You will still be enlisting. Dean Hauser is expecting you in her office at seven pm. She will explain everything then."

Dorene smiled. "But *you* have a basement to clean before you meet with Dean Hauser."

"Oh, yeah." Masha jumped up, barely able to contain herself. "Right away!" She turned back at the door, grinning from ear to ear. "Thank you, thank you both. This means... It means so much."

They waved her off.

"Nonsense!"

"This is what we do."

"Now go!"

Masha went.

CHAPTER TWENTY-TWO

Q BBS *Meredith Reynolds*, Etheric Academy, Alpha Class Dormitory

Yana was torn. She held up two dresses for Tina, Halli, and Mischa to judge.

"I cannot decide which one to wear for graduation," she told them. "I know it's only going under my robes, but I want to feel special."

"What about this one?" Tina dived into her closet, rummaged around, and held a dress up.

Yana made a moue. "It's a bit puffy."

Tina pulled out another. "How about this?"

Yana shook her head. "No, too blue. I'll look like an Alice."

That made Halli giggle. "I think you'd look more like Cinderella," she teased.

Yana huffed. "It cannot possibly be this difficult to choose a dress nobody will even see!"

Mischa looked up from filing her nails. "I know what we should do."

Tina, Halli, and Yana waited for her to reveal her solution.

Mischa smirked. "Let's go shopping!"

Masha returned from the bathroom. "Did I hear someone say shopping?"

"I can't think of a better way to spend our birthday, can you?"

"Besides," Yana added. "We have our final robe fittings later today, so we should make the most of the day. We should see what the boys are doing after we're done with the fitting."

Halli snickered. "The boys have planned their own day. It involves video games and pizza."

Tina looked over from where she was putting the dresses away. "Pizza? I could go for some pizza."

"It's not even lunchtime yet," Mischa exclaimed. "How can you think about pizza."

Tina shook her head sagely. "It's *pizza*. How could you not?"

QBBS *Meredith Reynolds*, Open Court, Arcade

"And the crowd goes wiiiiild!" Todd accompanied his victory yell with a lap of the floor.

Maxim shook his head at the younger boy's antics, putting his Coke down on the table. He spoke loudly for Craig to hear him over the noise of the arcade machines. "He reminds me of you. Same planet-sized ego and heart of gold."

Craig winked. "If you can back it up, there's nothing wrong with shouting about your awesomeness. That kid is a shit-hot pilot already. If I had a choice between big-head there and some stranger with all the ego and none of the skills, I know who *I'd* pick to fly me out of a war zone."

Nestor climbed out of the flight simulator with a face like thunder. "Hey, quit dancing! I want a rematch!" he yelled to Todd over the noise.

Craig nodded at Maxim's cousin. "Him, too. I was talking to a buddy of mine who works on the flight simulators and he said the two of them hold records that even the pros haven't been able to beat." He scratched his cheek absentmindedly. "So, how's your dad doing?"

Maxim grinned. "Really well. He's going to be out of Medical soon."

Craig clapped Maxim on the back in congratulations. "That's great, dude! Where will he be staying?"

"With my uncle, for now," Maxim told him. "When he's had time to adjust to station life he might get a place of his own."

Craig frowned. "You won't go with him?"

Maxim shook his head. "He doesn't want that. I told him I would defer my basic training to take care of him, but he refused outright. Said he would rather spend the rest of his life in Medical than negatively impact my future."

"Wow. That's like, deep, dude. But you have two months before then, right?"

Maxim nodded. "Yeah, Commander Silvers gave me the time to reconnect with my father. But it's graduation first, and I'm more nervous about that if I'm honest. I want my father to be there. And I feel stupid in the robe."

Craig jumped up and fished a tablet out of his fatigues.

"Hey, about that… I had a message telling me to report for a robe fitting. I already left the Academy, so why do I need robes?"

Maxim shrugged. "I have no idea. Did you ask?"

Craig shook his head.

"You wanna go and find out? I have a fitting later today. We all do."

Craig waved his tablet. "I'll ask Meredith."

Meredith's cool voice came from his speaker. "How can I help you, Craig?"

"Hey, Meredith. Do you know why I've been scheduled for a robe fitting today?"

There was a pause before Meredith answered. "You are scheduled to graduate tomorrow, Craig."

Craig frowned. "I thought I already graduated?"

"Technically, yes," Meredith replied. "But the Academy administrators insisted that you get to take part in the ceremony."

Maxim grinned. "The guys are going to love that. I'll make sure Dwayne gets a photo of you in your robe."

Ron and Aleksei came over with four baskets of buffalo wings. "What's that?"

Maxim pointed at Craig. "He gets to graduate with us tomorrow."

Ron high-fived Craig. "Awesome! So what do you guys want to do until then? I had a message from the girls saying they would be here shopping today. They want to know if we want to go for pizza after the fitting?"

Maxim scooped a wing from his basket. "Sounds good to me."

CHAPTER TWENTY-THREE

Q BBS *Meredith Reynolds*, **Open Court**

The seating area of Reap What You Sew was full of excited chatter since students from a few different schools were there, waiting their turn to have the final fittings for their graduation gowns.

Tina, Yana, Halli, and the twins had snagged a low couch in the corner by the store window so they could see when the boys arrived. The couch was an island in a sea of shopping bags of all sizes and colors.

Tina shook her head. "How are we going to get all this back to the Academy? We should get an antigrav pallet."

Mischa snickered. "We did more than retail damage today. It was more like retail annihilation. We should wait and see if the boys offer to help before we get a cart. It makes them feel needed."

Tina made a face. "Yeah, I don't think so."

"Shouldn't they already be here?" Halli fretted. She looked up as the bell over the door tinkled and Ksenia came in with Jaden and Kris. Ksenia made a point of glaring daggers at the twins before joining her friends. "Ugh."

"I know, right?" Masha agreed. "She gets on my last nerve. I don't even know what her problem is."

"I do," Tina told them in a hushed voice. "I overheard my mom saying that she couldn't accept Ksenia onto her staff because she wasn't the right fit. She recommended that she join DipCorps instead."

Masha made a face. "Oh, Misch. Poor you!"

Mischa smirked. "I'm heading into the shark tank. You don't think a little guppy like her is going to bother me?"

Tina dissolved into giggles, which spread until the five of them were reduced to clutching their middles, helpless to stop.

They were so busy laughing that none of them noticed Ron and Aleksei arrive.

"What's so funny?" Aleksei asked, picking his way through the bags to sit down on the couch.

Yana wiped a tear from her eye. "The idea of Mischa getting her hair wet!" She hooted.

The boys looked at each other and shrugged as a large group of students from another school exited the fitting rooms noisily.

"The others are here," Tina announced, looking out of the window as the noisy students filed out. Maxim and Craig stood to the side to let them out before coming into the store to join the others at the couch.

Tina raised an eyebrow at Craig. "Are you still on leave?"

Craig nodded. "I have until after graduation. Apparently I'm taking part even though I already left to join the

Guardians. Something to do with the administrators not wanting me to miss out on the experience? Commander Silvers agreed with them, so here I am."

A man holding a long tape measure came out from the fitting room. "Etheric Academy students? This way, please."

QBBS *Meredith Reynolds*, Etheric Academy, Lobby

Max pushed his cart through the lobby, heading for the auditorium to take care of last-minute preparations for tomorrow's graduation ceremony.

His thoughts were filled by the students who had come into this building as children and would leave tomorrow as adults.

How quickly time passed!

They had come such a long way since he'd brought them here on the Academy's opening day. The culmination of their growth appeared to have happened almost overnight.

He, smiled fondly, remembering Tina covering her nerves with snark, Yana's fear making her as quiet as a mouse, Ronnie's lack of confidence in himself. He remembered how the Romanovkan kids had barely spoken any English. Now they cursed as well as any of the others when they thought the adults weren't listening. He saw great things in Maxim's future especially.

He spotted little Bai Hu and Todd Grimes huddled over their tablets in their customary spot beneath the twinkling galaxy and called a greeting. The boys looked up and waved.

A chatter of giggling girls weighed down with

brightly-colored bags burst into the atrium from the main entrance, followed by the boys a few minutes later.

Max smiled warmly and trundled toward the auditorium as the future of the Empire piled into the lobby squabbling over who was to carry what.

Tina huffed as she hurried to catch up with the other girls before the door shut.

"Ugh, whose idea was it to build all these steps?" She didn't want to admit it, but she may have gone a little overboard with the retail therapy.

She sucked in a breath once she was safely through the door and reaffirmed her grip on her bags. Ron came up behind her and reached out to take her load, but she snatched the loot away. "I can carry my own things, thank you."

Ron held his hands up. "Only trying to help."

Tina smiled to show him she wasn't mad. "I've got it." She caught the door to the lobby with her shoulder and followed Halli and Yana inside.

Mischa held her bags out. "Here, Ron, you can carry mine if you like. I have no problem with chivalry." She dropped the bags at his feet and flounced out of the atrium and into the lobby.

Ron stood rooted to the spot with his mouth opening and closing.

Masha sashayed past and winked at him. "Wasn't quite the gesture you were going for, eh?"

Ron looked balefully at the masses of bags. "You could say that."

Masha walked through the doors, laughing and Ron closed his mouth as Maxim and Craig came up the steps with bags of their own.

"What have you got there, Ron?" Craig asked with a chuckle. "Looks a bit sparkly for your tastes."

Ron scowled as he struggled to pick up all the bags. "Mischa's swag, and why girls even need all this stuff is a mystery to me. I offered to take Tina's bags—don't ask me why when I should know better—and when she refused Mischa dumped all these on me."

Craig snickered and came forward to relieve Ron of his burden. "I'll take them. Where are the girls headed?"

Maxim gave Craig a questioning look. "You're ready to talk to Mischa?"

Craig shrugged and made his way to the others in the lobby.

"Oh, you made it." Tina blew out a breath and set off toward the stairs to the dorms. "Good. Now can we *please* dump our bags and get some dinner before the cafeteria closes for the night?"

Todd came over. "I asked Chef Van for takeout. We were just waiting for you to get here."

Tina dropped her bags and wrapped her arms around Todd in one fluid motion. "You are the best brother in the whole galaxy."

Todd squirmed free and turned back to Bai Hu. "You okay to finish up while I get the food?"

"Is it pizza?" Bai Hu asked.

Todd winked. "You know it is."

Bai Hu grinned. "Then I will wait here until you return. Meredith's update will be happening soon."

Todd returned to the lobby a short time later with a bag full of carry-out pizza boxes in each hand.

Bai Hu was just packing up when he reached their spot.

"You ready, buddy?" he asked.

Bai Hu nodded and slung his backpack over a shoulder. "There is something off with the galaxy tonight. Meredith must be busy, because it did not update at the expected time."

Todd glanced upward. "It didn't? Huh." He shrugged and held up one of his bags. "Let's go and eat. We'll come and see if it's updated on our way home."

Bai Hu looked one more time before following Todd up the stairs to the dorm.

The girls were by the sofa when Todd and Bai Hu got there.

Todd held the insulated bags aloft. "Pizza delivery, get 'em while they're hot!"

Tina threw the boots she was holding up to show Halli onto the sofa and rushed over to relieve Todd of the pizzas. Everyone came over to sit at the table while Tina shared the boxes out. The air was filled with a rich cheesy aroma and the sounds of a meal being enjoyed.

"How are you all feeling about tomorrow?" Todd asked between slices.

Tina grinned. "I feel like I want to sing and puke at the same time."

Halli pointed at Tina. "What she said. And I don't even have to give a speech!"

Tina paled. "My speech!"

Ron's mouth dropped open. "You didn't finish it?"

She shook her head.

Yana patted Tina's hand. "I will help."

"Yeah, me too," Ron told her.

"We can all help," Maxim added.

Todd stood up. "Sorry, sis, we've got to get back home soon, and we want to check on the galaxy before we leave." He came over to get a hug before heading for the door.

Yana ruffled Bai Hu's hair. "I will see you and Papa at the ceremony tomorrow, my little *kotenok*."

Bai Hu wrapped his arms around her middle and squeezed tight. "I will cheer loudly for you, *Jiějiě*."

———

The boys headed out of the dormitory wing and Bai Hu stopped at the top of the staircase and looked up. He grabbed Todd's arm and pointed at the galaxy projection, frowning. "Todd, look! It is frozen!"

Todd frowned as he squinted at the projection. "Has it crashed?"

Bai Hu nodded, letting his backpack slip from his shoulder so that he could rummage inside for his tablet. He brought up a timetable to show to Todd. "Look, the command center was due to send out the update over two hours ago."

"It comes from the command center? Why?" Todd asked.

Bai Hu looked at him in shock. "You did not know? The galaxy is one of the backups for the navigation display. If ours isn't working, maybe Admiral Thomas' is broken too."

Todd's frown deepened. "That's not good. We should tell someone."

Bai Hu nodded and called out. "Meredith?"

Meredith's voice came from Bai Hu's tablet. "Yes, Bai Hu, Todd. How can I assist you?"

Bai Hu leaned over the tablet. "The galaxy hasn't updated. Can you tell us why?"

"Are the main systems affected?" Todd asked.

Meredith replied a moment later. "The main systems were updated as scheduled. I can only assume there is a problem with the hardware in the projection room. I will alert Max."

"Thank you, Meredith," both boys chimed.

Max arrived a few minutes later, toolbox in hand. "Thanks for alerting us to the problem, boys. Meredith told me the projector was likely broken. Would you boys like to come with me to take a look?"

Bai Hu's eyes widened. "Go into the projection room? That is out of bounds."

Max's mustache fluffed out as his mouth opened wide in a grin. "Not if I permit you to be there, it isn't."

Max led the way up the stairs and into the library, taking them through the mesh gate into the restricted section.

"This is where we keep the books on how to blow things up," Max explained. "Makes no sense to leave that kind of thing lying about in a school full of geniuses."

He chuckled as he led them to the top of a spiral staircase where the door to the projection room lay behind a barred gate. Max flipped through the bunch of keys on this belt, selecting a medieval-looking one to insert into the heavy lock.

"Now, boys, mind you keep your hands to yourselves in here," Max told them. He placed his hand on a scanner mounted by the door and waited for it to turn green before pushing open the door with a flourish and standing back to let them drink it all in. "Welcome to the octagon, boys."

They entered what looked like a wide corridor, the inner wall ringed with windows spaced evenly.

Todd went to one of the windows and looked out on the frozen stars. At this near distance Todd could see every detail, the resolution of the projection crystal clear. "Hey, we're in the walls around the cupola!" He leaned back to touch one of the tiny projectors lining the edge of the window. "How many projectors does it take to make the galaxy?"

Max nodded and set off walking, gesturing for Bai Hu and Todd to follow. "If I recall correctly, there are over a thousand altogether."

They turned the corner and the outside wall was given over to blinking servers interspersed with control panels and monitor screens.

Bai Hu ran off along the corridor, examining the equipment with all the joy someone his age would usually reserve for a trip to the candy store. He scampered off to explore, calling out a few moments later. "I have found the problem."

A moment later Max and Todd caught up to Bai Hu, who stood in front of a bank of dark servers with a concerned expression on his face.

Todd gazed around without a clue what he was looking at. "What does all this stuff do?" he asked the custodian.

Max put his toolbox down on the floor. "The servers translate the scans we receive from the command center and transmit the data through the projection cameras as light. Looks like we have our fault. Let's see what the problem is, shall we?"

Bai Hu bent down next to the silent machine and held up a frayed cable. "This has been chewed," he told them. He sniffed at the cable. "By a rabbit."

Max did a double-take. "A rabbit? Are you sure?"

Bai Hu nodded. "I hunted rabbits for food back on the mudball, so I know the smell." His nose twitched. "I think it is still here." He sniffed again, moving his head until he caught the scent again. He pointed at the server. "It is inside!"

Max took a canvas bag from his toolbox and passed it to Bai Hu. "Okay, this is what we're going to do. Put that sack over your arms so you don't get scratched or bitten. I'm going to remove the casing and you're going to gently place the sack over the rabbit and scoop it up. Can you do that?"

Bai Hu nodded.

Max turned to Todd. "You wait behind Bai Hu in case the rabbit runs before he can secure it, got it?"

Bai Hu got into position and Todd crouched behind him like a quarterback waiting for the snap. Max pried open the casing on the server, taking care not to let the rabbit escape before they were ready. He slowly moved the front of the casing away and there the rabbit was, sitting hunched on a bundle of chewed wires in the corner of the server.

Bai Hu reached inside and popped the rabbit into the sack before it had a chance to react. He straightened up, handing the sack back to Max.

"Good job, boys." Max grinned, but his grin faded into a grimace when he bent to examine the chewed wires inside the casing, flipping the mass over with a gloved finger to reveal a sludgy puddle of rabbit waste. "But repairing the damage here is beyond my ability." He ran a hand over his head as he considered the best action. "Okay, boys, this is what we're going to do. I'm going to clean up here and get the rabbit over to the habitat. You two run and fetch Tina, Ron, and Aleksei. Tell them they can use anything they need from my tools to get the job done. If anyone can get the projector back up and running it will be those three."

CHAPTER TWENTY-FOUR

QBBS *Meredith Reynolds*, Etheric Academy, Lobby
Maxim and Craig stood with Masha and Mischa by the auditorium doors, handing out programs to people as they went inside.

"Where are they?" Maxim asked for the third time, fidgeting in his graduation gown. "They're going to miss the start."

A few stragglers milled in the center of the lobby, staring at the galaxy, which was still stationary.

Masha pointed up at the frozen projection. "They'll be here when *that's* back up and running. Diane and Dorene told them to take a break if they weren't finished, but you know those three."

Mischa snickered. "Like talking to a dead bear. No point."

The last few stragglers filed into the auditorium and Max came to check on them.

The custodian looked up at the still image. "Still nothing, huh?"

Maxim was about to offer to go up to the projection room and drag the three of them down to the ceremony whether they wanted to leave or not when the projection flickered and the galaxy overhead began its slow rotation once more.

"Woohooo!" Mischa cheered.

Max grinned and set off for the right-hand staircase. "Meredith has informed me that Tina, Ron, and Aleksei are ready to come down from the projection room. They'll be here soon, so you four go and take your places."

Tina tugged at her graduation gown, trying to remove the wrinkles she'd caused when she pulled it on hurriedly over her activewear. "So much for my outfit."

She ran lightly down the staircase, cutting across the lobby ahead of the boys, who were still wrestling with their gowns as they exited the library.

She slowed as she passed the auditorium doors to take her customary glance at the quote above them. She was pleasantly surprised to see that the quote had been changed. "How apropos for today."

Ron came to a stop beside her. "You have always loved the quotes."

Aleksei inserted himself between Tina and Ron, wrapping an arm around each. "If you two are having a moment, don't take too long. We're late enough as it is." He hurried inside the auditorium.

Tina took a step toward the doors and stopped. "This is

really it, isn't it? The end of the Academy for us, and the start of everything to come."

Ron placed a hand on her shoulder. "We've got this, Tina. Whatever comes."

She nodded once, then again more confidently. "Come on, then. Let's go."

They went inside and wove their way to the stage, where the rest of the graduating students were getting comfortable in fold-down chairs on the raised platform on either side.

Tina saw Yana wave from the opposite side and skirted the lectern in the center, pulling Ron up the steps by the arm. They scooted past Craig and Mischa, who sat together holding hands.

She took her seat beside Yana and scanned the audience, searching the front rows where the parents sat with the friends they'd made thanks to their children's friendships. Her mom was there in the first row, dabbing her eyes as Todd tried to console her. Maxim's uncle was next to her with Nestor beside him, and Yana's father sat with Bai Hu farther along the row with Masha and Mischa's parents.

She nudged Ron, nodding at the end of the second row where his parents were taking photo after photo of their son. "See, they do love you," she told him as they waved to him.

A couple of rows behind the families and friends of the graduating students, the Guardians had come out in force. They filled the middle of the auditorium and were providing most of the buzz. Tina saw Peter talking to Craig Senior. She was about to ask Masha if she could lipread their conversation when Maxim gasped beside her. He stood up and pointed at the auditorium's doors.

"He made it!"

Tina followed his finger, seeing an older version of Maxim coming through the door with a woman in a nurse's uniform supporting him.

Maxim held a hand over his mouth, uncaring of the tears that fell as every Guardian in the auditorium got to their feet and applauded his father.

Nikolai for his part was embarrassed, waving off the attention as he took a seat beside Peter. He met Maxim's gaze, holding a hand to his heart. "I am so proud of you, my son," he mouthed.

Maxim sat down, overcome with joy.

"It's all come together, hasn't it?" Tina marveled.

The next two hours passed in a blur as first Diane and then Dorene gave a speech, then the deans. Finally, various members of the faculty spoke and handed out achievement awards.

Too soon, it was Tina's turn to take the podium.

She looked at her mother in the audience for reassurance. Cheryl Lynn waved her mascara-stained handkerchief at Tina, her streaky face a picture of parental pride.

Tina took her cue cards out of her gown and stepped up to the microphone as the audience applauded.

She cleared her throat. "Thank you all for being here. This is a huge day for us all, the day we go our separate ways and take the next step." She looked down at her cards, suddenly hating everything she'd prepared to say.

She sighed and put the cards down on the lectern. "You

know, I had this whole monologue about the future planned, but I spent all of last night and most of today repairing a vital system and it put everything into perspective. Most of you won't know this, but I was the first kid to go into space. My mom wasn't too happy with Marcus for taking me up without asking, but that was the happiest moment of my life."

She saw Marcus sitting with the faculty and gave him a little wave. "That day, I saw the wonder of the galaxy in extreme close-up; possibilities beyond our comprehension. So how can we plan for a future when we know almost nothing about what lies ahead? We can't. Did everyone see the quote above the doors on the way in here?" She waited for a beat. "In case you missed it, it reads, *You cannot predict the future, but you can create it.*" She swept an arm to encompass all the students on the stage. "*We* are the future of your creation. I stand before you today to make that vow on behalf of everyone on this stage. It will be our honor, our duty, and our privilege to build upon what you, our parents and teachers, have given us, to use our knowledge in service of our Empress and our people, *ad aeternitatem!*"

The people in the audience all stood to clap and cheer and she stepped down to thunderous applause. Diane and Dorene came forward as Tina went back to her seat.

"Thank you for that rousing speech, Tina," Dorene enthused. She turned to the audience. "Tina Grimes, everybody!"

Diane held up her hands for quiet as they broke into a fresh ovation. "Thank you all. Our final speaker needs no introduction."

"In fact, we'd better get out of the way. We're in her spot."

Diane and Dorene vacated the stage and the applause died down as the lights dimmed. Lilting harp music began to play, and a hush blanketed the audience as the screen at the back of the stage began to glow faintly.

Tina looked at the side of the stage just in time to see Bethany Anne's guards fanning out to cover it. Bethany Anne stood in the wings with John and Ashur and winked when she saw Tina looking. Then she placed one hand on Ashur's back and the other on John's shoulder and all three disappeared.

So that's *how they do it,* Tina thought.

The music ceased, and the footlights threw up a spread of reds and blues to dance over the glowing screen.

A voice began to speak, reverberating around the auditorium. It was the voice of their Empress, and it filled them with its rightness.

"As long as a student pushes themselves, I'll turn over the heavens to help them."

The lectern in the center was suddenly illuminated and Bethany Anne stood there with Ashur at her side and John at her back.

The Empress adjusted the height of the microphone and rested her hands on the lectern. "It is with great pride I stand here today. Not so long ago, we made human history when we left Earth behind and crossed the Gate. We are here today to celebrate another momentous occasion—our children crossing the threshold into adulthood." She half-turned to take in the students on either side of her before facing the audience with a wry smile. "It's no secret that the greatest challenge with our inaugural class hasn't been getting them to push themselves, it's been keeping them alive long enough to reach that potential as they trampled over every boundary they came up against. When Alpha Class destroyed a chunk of the moon on their first class trip, we should have known there and then what to expect going forward from our most brilliant young minds."

There was a smattering of snickers from the audience.

She swept a finger across the rows of parents. "*You* raised them to give their best, and *Gott Verdammt* but they ran with that from the minute they arrived. They have outstripped every expectation we had for them, and I have faith that they will continue to do so. Not despite the challenges we have ahead of us, but because of them. This Academy was founded on the principle that our brightest and best would be given the freedom to grow and explore their burgeoning talents in a nurturing environment, regardless of where they came from back on Earth. I want to thank the entire faculty, past and present—yes, even you, Bobcat—for the knowledge you have shared with these fine young men and women."

Bethany Anne smiled as the audience chuckled and many turned to see Bobcat blushing. She let it die down before addressing the students.

"That knowledge is the foundation on which our strength rests and the armor that protects us against the onslaught. And make no mistake—it *will* be an onslaught. We came to make war, and the war has already begun. Destroying injustice wherever it rears its ugly-ass head will not be quick, nor will it be easy."

There was a gasp as Bethany Anne's hair rose to float

around her head. Her eyes blazed red, bathing the people in the front rows in their glow.

"We will fight and bleed, and we will sacrifice to wrest control of this galaxy—*our* galaxy—back from the Kurtherians. We will protect our home and ensure the safety of our people. I refuse to lie to you; it's going to be *damn hard*. But it's also going to be an adventure. You are the pioneers, the next wave of our military, our scientists and engineers, our envoys to the galaxy and beyond. I am incredibly proud to know that every single one of you sitting before me now is not only capable in your field, but willing to go above and beyond. With men and women like you making up the backbone of the Empire, humanity will do much more than survive the wars ahead."

Her eyes flashed again, and her voice emanated from everywhere in the auditorium.

"We will prevail."

The End

Nat's Author Notes – Alpha Class: Graduation

I can't believe I'm at this point again! Thank you SO MUCH for reading my second book! The training wheels were definitely taken off with this one, and I hope you enjoyed it!

So many exclamation marks. What can I say, I'm an excitable person ;)

I am a proper author now. I almost started again at least three times while I was writing this book. It had SIX sets of beats before I was satisfied that I'd covered every open arc, and a week ago I totally rewrote the whole book. No exaggeration. It was SO important to me that I lived up to the high praise you all heaped on Discovery. Luckily, I have such wonderful family and friends that the pressure I put on myself to make sure that this book closed out the story in a way that made YOU happy wasn't that bad, and here we are!

Gratitude bombs!

Thank you to my family – both by blood and by love. Every single one of you deserves so much more than a simple thank you in a book! Especially you, Stevie. There aren't enough words.

Thank you to Michael, as always, for having faith in me. I am just one of a multitude of people whose life is so much better for having you in it, whether directly or indirectly. Also to Lynne for allowing me to distract her literally all the time (which is my polite way of saying I bug her constantly), and for curing me of my commaitis (not in author notes though, hahaha!) We're working on the unnecessary gerunds.

To my beta team – who are also my bestest of friends, and everyone from JIT for their hard work and dedication in helping me get this book as perfect as possible. Also to the people who work tirelessly behind the scenes to make us all look good. Tabitha, you are literally the most lovely person and I love having you around! His Zen-ness Steve Campbell who makes me look awesome, and Karla Kay for the wiki that enables me to dip in and out of the main KG arc and weave it all together without spelling the names wrong.

Last but not least, thank *you*! Thank you to everyone for all the love and enthusiasm you've sent my way. I've had the best experience as a new author and I'm so utterly grateful for my community. Much love to everyone in the Facebook groups! You all keep me sane while I'm writing and human contact is at a minimum. There is always someone there, no matter what time of day (and usually night) with a meme, or a chat, and I appreciate you all! You can stop with the donut pics now though, they are

NOT helping me resist! (PBTD group, I'm looking at you! ;))

Graduation, and beyond

So that's it. The end of the *Alpha Class* story! The kids are kids no more. How do you feel about that? Definitely come and tell me about it! You can leave a review on Amazon, and you can also find me in the Kurtherian Gambit Facebook groups (links at the bottom as always). I don't want you to be too sad. You already know where Tina ends up, and you'll be happy to know that this isn't the end for most of the others, either! You all know I love a good cameo (hey, I'm still a fan!) and this book had a *very* special appearance. More about that shortly...

First, a big long waffle to get to it (please, you didn't think I *wasn't* going to waffle? It's like you don't even know me!) If you have just picked up this book randomly, drawn in from the main KG series by Jeff Brown's beautiful cover (this is my favourite cover of the four, I love it!) then go back and read from the beginning! This little corner of KG has its own story.

Cue suspenseful music...

It began long, long ago... Not really. It's been less than two years since Michael brought Scott (TS) Paul onboard to start the Etheric Academy series. But in Kurtherian Gambit terms it's an eternity. Scott wrote two books that we all loved. So much so, that one of the most frequent posts in the fans group was to ask when the next one would be available. As a fan, I was devastated when I learned that he was unable to complete the story, even though I understood the reasons. So when I 'graduated' (see what I did there?) from Fans Write and Michael gave me the option I jumped on the chance to complete his story, and Scott has been a total legend throughout the whole thing. (Thank you, Scott! I wish you even more success than you're already having!)

Discovery was the fastest book I've written (three weeks) and *Graduation* has been the longest so far (Was it like eight, or something? Nine? **Too many** weeks!!!) Finishing a series is complicated. Not only was it the bigger challenge, I had another level up in skill and knowledge because I started editing for Lynne. I am *beyond* lucky that I get to learn from Lynne. She's an actual genius with language and also a complete treasure. I've learned so much in the last two months that is going to make your experience as a reader better.

Writing Graduation went a bit like this...

-Write

-Learn something

-Rewrite that last bit, which looked good last week but is *so* not good now I know the new thing

...aaand repeat. Totally worth it. Love you, Lynne! **(Bows in awe)**

Reviews. Thank you so much to everyone who reviewed *Discovery*! Even the ones who gave less than five stars. I appreciate all honest feedback and take it all into consideration. However, I cannot make these books longer than they're supposed to be. There was a template, it was 50k, and I stuck to it to keep continuity across the series. YA is not 80k words like the BA books.

But my next series will be...more in line with expectations.

(And we're almost back at the cameos now, well done for hanging in there!)

Next for me is *Holi's War*, which is the continuation of the story that started Fans Write, *Holi's Savior*. You can find that story in *Fans Write Volume 1*–along with the prequel to the next brand new and shiny Kurtherian Gambit series I'm going to tell you about *right now*. Did you notice a change in tone during the scene with Anna Elizabeth Hauser? That's because I didn't just have a character cameo in this book...I had an *author* cameo! I co-wrote that scene with my very good friend Sarah (SE) Weir—you all just got a sneaky peek into her upcoming series *The Empress's Spy*! And that's all I'm saying. You'll have to wait...but not for long!

In the meantime, I'm getting ready to cross an ocean! Vegas, baby!! I'll be at the 20Books Vegas convention in November, along with the other two-thirds of my coven...ahem...the Sisters Three, Sarah (SE) Weir and Erika Everest. If you read Michael's notes in *Payback is a Bitch* then you'll know that he invited the **whole of fandom** to Vegas on the 8th (you just have to love that!!) It's a perfect opportunity to come and say hi and get us authors to sign your stuff while you pelt us with questions. I hope to see you there! Please leave your pitchforks at home though, yes? (**snicker**)

So, I think I've said it all. Except, for the final time on this series,

Ad Aeternitatem,
Nat

JUNE 10, 2018

First, THANK YOU for not only reading this story, but these author notes as well!

My author notes will be a bit shorter. Due to scammers and stuffers trying to do ugly things to game the system, Amazon has needed to setup a rule that no more than 10% of a book should be bonus material.

(I'm happy about that!)

So, I'm going to keep my author notes rather short and say that I appreciate all of you that have supported Scott (TS) Paul and Natale Roberts with the Etheric Academy series.

As Natale mentioned, Scott has been super helpful even though his time is at a premium as well because he is running his own publishing company (all while writing his own stories.)

I reached out to Scott to ask him what title would be best if you haven't read any of his non-Kurtherian books and he suggested *Conjuring Quantico*, the first book of his best-selling *The Federal Witch* urban fantasy series. You can click to find it on a local Amazon website here:

http://www.books2read.com/conjquantico

A little over two and a half years ago I was basically working alone, had a few fans on Facebook and Amazon (when we could chat on Amazon), and had no idea who Natale Roberts was. Scott would enter my life about January of 2016 or so.

Due to that friendship, he would go on to produce the first two books in this series before *Federal Witch* blew up so big that he had to go head down, fingers flying to produce the next book in the series...

And the next one, and the next one ;-)

However, because of Scott, we were blessed to get the first two books in this series that fans have loved.

However, the story needed to be completed. I appreciate Natale stepping up that one day when I asked if she would be willing to finish the series (I had already confirmed with Scott he would not be able to get back to it.)

Having Scott help Natale is a godsend, since he takes meticulous notes about his stories and his plans. Basically, he is a much better documentarian with his Universes than I have ever been.

Now we finish with this set of the *Etheric Academy*. It was always designed to be a way to continue with additional classes and perhaps in the future we will see what goes on with other students.

But, that will have to be another time. For now, we just got finished with *Graduation*, and it's SUMMER TIME!

(No, it actually is, note the date I'm typing this. MANY students all across America (at least) just got out of school for summer.)

Coincidence?

Maybe.

I'd like to finish with letting you know something that is a bit behind-the-scenes. Natale is every bit as nice and sweet working with her as she is out on Facebook with the Fans Write efforts. (Editor's note: She really is!)

Perhaps even more so (since she prefers to be in the background like most authors.)

BUT – she doesn't like waiting for information WHAT-SOEVER. *It drives her nuts,* and she will weasel it out of you when you are not looking or paying attention.

I can't give you examples, but suffice it to say…

I'm ON to you, Natale! ;-)

That 'large eyes looking for help' routine won't get you what you want for the tenth time in a row.

I don't think.

Ad Aeternitatem,
Michael

P.S. – If you missed the TS Paul book link above (because you continued reading my amazing *Author Notes*) here it is again:

http://www.books2read.com/conjquantico

Jack Dalton Book 7

Jack Dalton Book 8

Jack Dalton Book 9

Jack Dalton Book 10

Magical Division Origins

Jack Dalton, Monster Hunter Box Set (1-3)

Jack Dalton, Monster Hunter Box Set (4-6)

Jack Dalton, Monster Hunter Box Set (7-10)

Jack Dalton Monster Hunter: The Complete Collection (Books 1-10)

Athena Lee Chronicles

The Forgotten Engineer

Engineering Murder

Ghost Ships of Terra

Revolutionary

Insurrection

Imperial Subversion

The Martian Inheritance - Audio Now Available

Infiltration

Prelude to War

War to the Knife

Ghosts of Noodlemass Past

Forgotten Hope

Athena Lee Universe

Shades of Learning

Space Cadets

The Federal Witch: The Collected Works, Book 1

Chronicles of Athena Lee Book 1-3

Chronicles of Athena Lee Book 4-6

Chronicles of Athena Lee Book 7-9 plus the prequel

New Beginnings

Kutherian Gambit

Alpha Class. The Etheric Academy book 1

Alpha Class - Engineering. The Etheric Academy Book 2

The Etheric Academy (2 Book Series)

WANT MORE KURTHERIAN GAMBIT?

Join the Kurtherian Gambit email list here: http://kurtherianbooks.com/email-list/

Join the Kurtherian Gambit Facebook Group Here: https://www.facebook.com/TheKurtherianGambitBooks/